Charlotte Calder was born in Adelaide and grew up in the Adelaide Hills and Darwin. She has worked as, among other things, an actor and a photographer and has written occasional columns for the *Sydney Morning Herald* and the *Australian*. Her first novel, *Settling Storms*, was published in 2000.

Charlotte lives with her husband and three children, aged seventeen, sixteen and ten, in the central west of New South Wales. She loves white cockatoos, emails, cats, dogs, horses, trips to Sydney, and most other things that distract her from getting on with her next novel.

CUPID PAINTED BLIND

Charlotte Calder

PAN
Pan Macmillan Australia

First published 2002 in Pan by Pan Macmillan Australia Pty Ltd
St Martins Tower, 31 Market Street, Sydney

National Library of Australia
Cataloguing-in-Publication data:

Calder, Charlotte.
Cupid painted blind.

For young teenagers.
ISBN 0 330 36373 5.

1. Electronic mail messages – Juvenile fiction. 2. Teenage
girls – Juvenile fiction. 3. Interpersonal relations in
adolescence – Juvenile fiction. I. Title.

A823.4

Set in 12.5/14.5 pt ApolloMT by Midland Typesetters,
Maryborough, Victoria
Cover model: Katherine Gallagher
Printed in Australia by McPherson's Printing Group

To my mum, Chibby, with
much love

CHAPTER 1

sefi_15 <do u believe in true love?>
tupper_wez <if she's good looking>
piachicki <i suurrlee do>
annidreama <trust u, toad>
ToMtOm <if she was good looking it wouldnt be mutual, thats 4 sure>
tupper_wez <sez who?>
piachicki <sez all of us, cuddly one!>
p_a_k <hey - anybody going to the something for kate concert?>
annidreama <why, anyone speshul in mind?>
p_a_k <u shouting??>
annidreama <not you, dummy. have u fallen in lurve or somefink sefi?>
sefi_15 <who ME?>
tupper_wez <gonna roll right over yas>
tupper_wez <1 roll & i squash intellectual pygmies>

annidreama <yeah u>

tupper_wez <& stick insects>

piachicki <well roll away then - off the screen>

p_a_k <like - terror!>

tupper_wez <yes winged ant - i go>

tupper_wez left the room

p_a_k <don't go bruvver - all is forgiven>

piachicki <hey - didn't mean it>

piachicki <hope he's not all poopy>

ToMtOm <nah - hes got a geography assignment due last week>

annidreama <he knows we luv im>

annidreama <the great hairy git>

sefi_15 <don't remind me - assignments>

annidreama <well if nobodys got anything sciiintillllating 2 say>

annidreama <gtg 2>

piachicki <ditto - fossils screaming>

p_a_k <hey - wot if we opened this up>

p_a_k <like, made it an open chat room?>

sefi_15 <tell me about it - mine's frothing at the mouth!>

ToMtOm <???)-:>

annidreama <why wld we wanna do that?!>

piachicki <no WAY, we'd get every weirdo in cyberspace>

sefi_15 <jus wouldnt be US anymore!!>

p_a_k <ok ok just asking>

annidreama <well don't ask again, shitferbrains>

sefi_15, aka Persephone Harkness, jabbed at the modem button and cancelled the connection. Goodbye friends, hello desktop. The icons were now hardly visible against the rearing outlines of the giant fighting stag beetles her little sister Hedy had insisted on pasting as wallpaper.

She picked up her fork and pushed cold pillows of ravioli about the half-eaten bowl on her lap. Her battered school copy of Shakespeare's *A Midsummer Night's Dream* sat beside the monitor, unopened and accusing.

'Seph?' Her mother Susan's voice came floating up from the bottom of the stairs. "I hope you've just about finished – I need the computer now!'

Finished?! Furiously she double-clicked on 'Documents'. Dingly ding: the stag beetles bugged off.

And there it was – the document in question. Joke. What there was of the document. 'A Midsummer Night's Nightmare'. Right at the top of the screen where she'd left it, an hour and a half ago, before the lure of the login became too great.

She groaned and snatched up the book, flipping through the pages in the vain hope that some gorgeous, wonderful kid from a bygone year had just happened to scribble the entire essay topic down a margin.

'*Seph* – did you hear me?'

'*Finished*? I'm not nearly finished, Mum!' Her heart was starting to race. There was nothing, of course, in those worn, musty-smelling pages but underlinings, illegible scribbles and a heart or two, pencilled in with the usual lovelorn initials.

Just pages and pages of the bloody play itself, great slabs of olde verse, lofty and dense, full of thous and thines and wilts and mines . . .

'It's been taking me hours!' she cried. 'Why can't you use your laptop?'

Susan's footstep creaked ominously on the stairs.

'I told you – there's been something wrong with the disk drive. It's coming back from the repair place tomorrow. Now no arguments, Persephone. Five more minutes and then I've *got* to start my report.'

Seph frantically double-clicked, and there it was:

Themes of Love and Unreality in 'A Midsummer Night's Dream'

by Persephone Harkness

'And I've got to hand in this essay tomorrow or I'll lose twenty per cent – straight off!' Tears welled suddenly in Seph's eyes as her whole one line of work blurred tragically across the screen:

Love and the unreality of love are the main themes in Shakespeare's 'A Midsummer Night's Dream' because

Blank.

Too late now to sneak out to the video store and grab the movie version . . . wasn't it?

'Well you've had all afternoon to do it – what on *earth*'ve you been doing?'

Silence. As Hedy would say: 'Warning! Danger zone ahead!'

4

'It's just so hard, Mum. It's taken me *ages* to write it . . .'

And the time just goes so fast in the chat room and I even talked to him on my own for a little while; fat lot of good it did me . . .

'. . . and I just need a bit more time – *please*? Just another half an hour?'

'Look, it's nine-fifteen and I've got three hundred delegates to speak to first thing in the morning!' There was a loud sigh, another step up. 'What's the essay about? Can *I* help you?'

'*No*! I mean . . . it wouldn't be all my work then, would it?'

'You'll just have to *write* it out, in longhand.'

'I can't do that!'

'Why on earth not? It's all I ever did when I was your age. We certainly didn't have computers!'

'Mrs Ahern can't read my writing! And anyway, why can't you?'

'What?'

'Write *yours* out by hand? I was here first.'

Oh-oh. Bad mistake, Seph, bad mistake.

'*Persephone Harkness*, you get off that computer and go to your own room right now, or you'll be grounded for a month! And I know perfectly well you've been wasting time in those damn chat rooms – I wasn't born yesterday!'

'I have *not*.'

Give up, Seph, quit while you're ahead. You'll just have to try and write out something by hand. But what? Why the hell didn't you pay more attention during the class reading?

She sighed. 'Okay Mum, just saving it to disk.'

She clicked back to 'Files', highlighted 'Midsummer Night's Nightmare'.

Then pressed 'Delete', and destroyed the evidence.

———

'By hand, Seph?' Mrs Ahern looked up at Seph from her desk, her eyebrows lifting quizzically. 'That must've been a hardship.' She peered down through her enormous glasses at the essay. 'Well, I hope I'm going to be able to read it.'

Seph shrugged and smiled weakly.

'Me too.'

In a way, she thought, it'd be better if Mrs A couldn't read it. Seph's attempt at speed reading a whole Shakespearean play at ten o'clock on a Sunday night had been a complete failure. All those woods and silvery moons and weird names (how on earth could you imagine a hero called Lysander – it sounded like a toilet cleaner), and she'd had to keep going back to the beginning just to find out who was falling in and out of love with who. It was totally confusing. First there was Hermia who was meant to be marrying Demetrius even though she was on with Lysander, and then there was Hermia's friend Helena who was in love with Demetrius who couldn't stand the sight of her. There was a whole lot of crazy chasing going on around the forest, interspersed with some country yokels making up a play, and the naughty fairy called Puck who went around squeezing magic juice in people's eyes so they'd get confused and suddenly get the hots for the wrong person.

Hardly 'love and unreality' – it was more like mega-embarrassing passion and total insanity!

Too late to ring friends for help, and of course with Susan hogging the computer she couldn't even get stuff from the Net. In the end she'd cobbled together something pathetic from the three or four pages of introduction at the front of the book, changing words wherever she could so it wouldn't end up looking like a complete steal. Padded out with crap like 'the unpredictability of love down through the ages . . .'

And lots of quotes, including the oh-so-famous one about 'the course of true love never did run smoothly'. Gave her a bit of a shock to see it right there in the first act – fancy old Bill Shakespeare being the first to think that one up. A total cliche nowadays, but still true.

Maybe that's why in her case, she thought, things hadn't really got started. It was just the slow, bumpy bit to begin with.

And then Susan'd burst in and said did she have any idea of the time and to get into bed immediately. Then this morning she'd meant to get up early and finish it off but Hedy had woken her up at five-thirty creeping round in her wardrobe looking for some jelly babies Hedy reckoned Seph'd pinched, and by the time she'd yelled at Hedy to get out and got back to sleep again, she was so tired she'd slept through the alarm at six.

She walked back to her desk, rolling her eyes at Pia as she went. Sometimes life was just too difficult. And there was still that maths to do by fifth period. She'd have to tackle it in the library at lunchtime.

But at lunch she'd just plonked herself down at a table by the window and was starting on the first question when there was a tickle of plastic on the tip of her nose, and Pia was standing there with Melissa, waving her internet card. 'We'll be at computer number eleven,' she sang, 'checking emails.'

'You go,' said Seph. 'I just have to do this maths, or Dawson'll chuck a spak.'

But when she looked up two minutes later and saw them hunched over a screen, grinning, it was all too much. Before she knew it she'd pushed out her chair and was across the library, peering around the corner of the screen.

'What've you got?'

'It's from Pak,' said Pia. She put a hand over her mouth and snorted.

'Shh!' hissed Melissa loudly. Over at the front desk Ms Battaglia looked up from her box of disks. All three straightened their expressions and gazed solemnly at the interesting information on the screen in front of them:

<hey girls:
we reckon the tupper ware is getting it on with
this old chick who works in the dining room
called rosita, cos she always gets him extra
helping of all his favourites like rhubarf crumble
and rice pudding, cos that's the way to his heart —
thru his stomach>

'Gross!' laughed Seph.

'Who's Tupper Ware?' Melissa gripped Pia's shoulder and leant so far forward she nearly toppled over.

'Y'know, Wez?' said Pia. 'The big fattish guy with the curly hair – the really funny one?'

Melissa looked blank.

Pia sighed, tapping her own forehead. 'Wez, short for "Ware"? Tupper, Andrew Tupper.'

Melissa's whisper morphed into a shout.

'Oh *that* guy. The one who fell into the pool that day before the races had even started?'

'*SHH*!'

Followed by the inevitable blast from the front desk. '*Girls*, there are people in here trying to *study*, thank you!'

'Yes, Ms Battaglia.'

Ms Battaglia's seachlight stare raked the rest of the library before settling back to her disks. Seph scanned the rest of the message.

<tom says g'day and do y'all wanna meet in the
city this arvo – how about at cappos round about
4?? warning – wez might bring the beootiful
rosita let us know,
pak>

Pia looked questioningly at Seph, who shrugged and tried to look nonchalant. Just the mention of his name was enough to start something fluttering in her throat. Could he possibly be meaning her especially, she wondered, or just everyone . . .

Then she remembered something, and lost it. Gave a little scream: 'Oh *no,* I've just remembered I promised Mum I'd collect Hedy from after-school care this afternoon!'

She clapped her hand to her mouth; there was dead silence. The air conditioning hummed faintly; a chair scraped. Nobody dared even peek in Battaglia's direction.

But there was no angry response from the desk – she must've toddled off. After a while Melissa whispered hoarsely, 'Can I come?'

For a split second Seph's and Pia's eyes met; a small current of irritation ran between them.

'Sure,' said Pia. She turned back to Seph.

'Can't you get out of collecting Hedy?'

Seph slowly shook her head. Stupid question. They knew Susan.

Suddenly she was on the verge of tears. She took a deep, quavery breath.

'Mum's got some stupid conference on,' she said. 'Work practices, or something.' Or some other equally hell-boring topic.

'Well then,' said Pia brightly, 'you'll just have to pick up Hedy, won't you, and bring her along with you into town.'

Hedy leant across the iron lacework table to Pak, her face flushed and damp in the late afternoon heat. 'You've got a lot of pimples,' she said. 'Why don't you use Clearasil, like Seph?'

'*Hedy*!' Seph turned on her sister, feeling sick. From across the footpath came a squeal of brakes; a car horn blared. 'Do you *mind*?'

But Hedy was away. 'Seph uses an *awful* lot of Clearasil,' she told all them gaily, her eyes shining. 'The white kind. Sometimes she puts it on so thickly when she goes to bed, Mum calls her The Ghost.'

Everybody except Seph laughed and guffawed so loudly that Hedy looked as though she was about to stand up on the seat to give an encore. But then her expression suddenly changed.

'Ow, Seph!' she squealed. 'Let go of my arm!'

'Well,' murmured Seph, gritting her teeth, 'shut *up* then.' She shrugged and tried to laugh at everyone, her face burning. The pimple on her chin was glowing, she knew, like a Santa's nose.

Dearest, darling little Hedy. Office workers streamed past the pavement cafe in a warm haze of dappled sun and traffic fumes, homeward bound, jackets slung over their shoulders. Seph just wished she could get up and melt away with them.

And Wez was egging Hedy on. He leant over his plate, empty now except for a circle of beetroot and some lettuce.

'So what else does she get up to? Tell us, kid!'

He grinned at Seph, who reached over and threatened to thump him.

'No violence at Cappo's!' He laughed, raising his arm against her. 'Come on, Hedy, spill!'

'We-ell . . .' Hedy took a deep, important breath.

But Melissa was practically shooting up her hand.

11

'You should hear her singing Abba songs in the shower!' She rolled her eyes at Pia. 'Remember, at camp last year?'

Seph stared at her, speechless, just as Tom asked: 'Does she talk in her sleep?'

Seph whirled around; he was smiling his slow smile at her. Her blush got worse; her face felt as though it was about to blow apart. She swallowed.

'None of your business.'

In her confusion there was nowhere to look but down. Her finger traced a trail through the dusting of tree spores on the table.

Why, she wondered, did he ask that?

Then she realised that beside her The Mouth was off again: '. . . *screams* out things in her sleep! You should hear her. The other night Mum thought there must have been a burglar in her room!'

Another pause. Hedy's gaze was positively drinking in her audience. 'Something about a solid wall. She kept on shouting "He can't see me!" '

Her ensuing yell caused several passing heads to turn, but Seph was by now past caring. She'd seized Hedy's elbow, fingernails digging into the plump flesh. She thrust her face in her sister's wide, freckled one, getting a waft, despite the traffic and pavement smells, of that familiar Hedy aroma of salty skin and bubble gum.

'If you say *one more word*,' she hissed, 'we're outa here! And I'll never pick you up from after-school care again – understand? You can stay there forever for all I care!'

Hedy's enormous eyes stared back at her.

'Now sit there and *shut up*!' Seph finished, her eyes

boring into her sister's. Then she remembered herself and turned to the others with a shrug and a 'what can you do?' kind of laugh.

They were all staring at her.

'Whew,' said Pak, pretending to wipe his brow. 'Glad you're not my sister. I'd be shit-scared!'

'Reckon!' Pia, squashed up next to Tom on the bench, was leaning against him, collapsing with laughter.

'Honestly, Seph, I didn't know you could be so *frightening*!'

Her long fingernails were sliding down his shirt; her teeth flashed in her wide mouth.

Tom reddened slightly and laughed. He looked sideways at Pia's blonde head bobbing on his shoulder, smelling deliciously, Seph knew, of Dazzling, or Blue Ocean, or one of the other perfumes on Pia's crowded dressing table. And Seph felt a tiny twist of fear.

Now Pia was turning and looking at Tom, smiling right into his eyes. 'You've got some cappuccino froth on your nose,' she said. And reached up with her little finger and wiped it off.

'Oh yuk, Pia!' shouted Hedy. 'You'll catch something!'

Pia, ever the funny flirt, laughed, and turned around to say something to Wez. But Seph was watching Tom.

He was just sitting there, gazing at the back of Pia's head.

And Seph tried to laugh along with whatever it was that Wez was saying, but suddenly she'd never felt more miserable in her life.

Later, when their cups were well and truly empty and Leonie the waitress was starting to give them Looks, Wez suddenly leant right out into the footpath and whistled loudly.

'*Simon*!' he yelled. 'Eh, Sim!'

Again heads turned, and Seph and Pia muttered, 'We-ez, d'you mind?' But a tall boy in a Grammar blazer had turned around and was looking in their direction. He gave a smile of recognition and started to duck back through the crowd.

'It's Simon,' Wez told them. 'Simon Yates – Annie's brother!'

'Is *he* her brother?' asked Pia. Her smile got bigger; she slid a hand across her mouth. 'He doesn't look a bit like Annie!'

Simon was powerfully built, with square-jawed good looks.

'He's only her half-brother,' said Tom coolly. 'He lives over in Clover Bay with his dad.'

For a moment they'd forgotten Tom had lived next door to their friend Annie, 'annidreama' in the chat room, since the year dot. Tom and Annie were probably closer than Simon and Annie had ever been.

Simon had reached their table. Wez stood up and clapped him on the back. 'Simmo, old son! Come and join us for a spot of refreshment!'

Simon looked uncertainly at them, jam-packed into the benches. He saw Tom and nodded. Then he spied Pia.

'Closing in three minutes,' sang Leonie, reaching over and swiping at the next table with a cloth. The tables had just about emptied. Mr Cappolucci, the owner, was starting to stack benches and lug them inside.

Wez twisted around. 'Ah, come on, Leonie. Just a teensy-weensy cappuccino?' He looked enquiringly at Simon. 'Or a flat white? And tell you what,' he added, magnanimously, 'you can bring me an almond croissant. Rosita's not on tonight – I don't wanna starve.'

'In your dreams, Wez,' said Leonie cheerfully. 'You're fat enough, and I got a class to get to by six-fifteen.'

Pak looked at his watch. 'Speaking of time, we gotta get back to school. The Turnip'll go ape if we're late for dinner again.'

But Wez had grabbed Leonie's skinny arm and taken her hand, cloth and all, in his two great paws. 'Ah, Leonie, me darlin', why are you so cruel to me, when you know how I lust after your tiny bod?'

Leonie yanked her hand free. 'Hey,' she grinned, flicking at his face with the cloth. 'Pick on someone your own size!'

'Anyway,' laughed Pak, 'where I come from they don't let elephants out on dates!'

There was a small silence, before cries of '*oooh*!' and 'nas-*ty*!'

Sometimes Pak could go a bit far, thought Seph, glancing sidelong at Wez. Was that a hint of hurt in his eyes?

But Wez was already on the comeback trail. He leant over to Pak.

'Where *you* come from, sonny boy, elephants stomp on midgets like yourself.'

'Yay, Wez!' cried Seph. 'Touché!' said Simon.

Pia slipped her arm around Wez's shoulder. 'Anyway,' she smiled, leaning in close, 'elephants would have to be my *favourite* animal!'

A spot of pink had formed on both her cheeks; light swam gold through her pigtails.

Simon, mouth open slightly, was staring at her. Then he cleared his throat and smiled reluctantly.

'Well, guess we'd better split. Do the coffee next time. Catch ya,' he added, his eyes meeting Pia's, 'later.'

He stood up, picked up his bag, gave a little wave and set off into the crowd again.

Pia, chin still on her hand, gazed at his retreating figure and smiled dreamily. 'Hope so,' she murmured. 'Gee, I hope so . . .'

'Oh-oh,' grinned Pak, and Wez shook his head.

'He's in Year 12, kid, much too old for you.'

Pia raised her eyebrows and smiled haughtily.

'Actually, he'd be *just* my mental age,' she said. 'Didn't you know that teenage boys are supposed to be two years behind girls in maturity?'

Loud scoffing from the boys.

'So *that*,' Pia continued sweetly, 'makes *you* lot, in Year 11, actually a year behind us girls!' When the carry-on had died down she added, 'Anyway, he seems just right to me!'

Seph saw Tom look down at his plate, twisting his knife handle between finger and thumb.

And she decided right then and there that her life was over.

Leonie was making furious calculations on her pad.

She tore it off and slapped the docket down. 'Thirty-seven thirty, thanks, guys, and I'm outa here.'

'Thirty-seven dollars!' croaked Melissa.

Seph muttered, 'Some of us just had coffee, not three-course banquets.'

Her face felt as though it was beginning to set, hard and cracked, like papier-mâché.

'Well some of us have to go back and face boarding school slop, not home-cooked dinners,' said Pak. He pulled out his wallet, looking at the bill. 'Here, I'll pay ten of it – I'm feeling generous. The old man just sent my allowance.'

'So much for the Asian slowdown,' said Wez.

Pia was counting out some coins; she glanced at her watch. 'Yikes, Mum'll be home by now, chucking a psych.'

Then she swung around to Tom.

'Eh, Kranowski, you catch the 265 up Wilton Road, don't you?'

Seph could hardly bear to see what she was sure was hope kindling in Tom's eyes.

'Uh huh,' he replied, starting to smile.

Pia reached behind for her blazer, lacy bra straining visibly through her shirt. She smiled back at him.

'Well then, what're we waiting for?'

Only for me to kill you, Pia, thought Seph, her heart constricting painfully as Tom gave Pak some money and stood up to follow Pia.

Only for me to kill you!

17

CHAPTER 2

That evening Seph went to her room and threw herself into her neglected homework. If you're feeling sick with misery, she figured, you might as well be doing quadratic equations. And anyway, she couldn't possibly hand it in late again.

Factorise: $2x^2 + x - 1 = 0$

Just forget Tom, she told herself. Forget them all – they could have one another for all she cared. She was now going to concentrate on becoming a brain. Brains didn't need boys; they just sailed on through in a cloud of brilliance and when they graduated with perfect scores and had unis all around the country begging them to enrol in astrophysics or cosmology, then all the Toms of the world would be shaking their heads and sighing, 'God, she's stunning. Missed our chance – guess she's lost to us forever now . . .'

Seph chewed on her pen and stared down at the page, but all she could see was the two of them vanishing into the crowd together, Pia touching his arm and laughing. And him following her like a lamb.

And suddenly Seph wondered if she really was going to be sick.

$10x^2 - 13x + 4 = 0$

A Midsummer Night's Dream was still sitting there on her desk, the pages all puffy between the covers, as though someone had once left it out in the rain. She'd have to read it properly. Mrs A wouldn't stand for any more shitty essays like the one she'd handed in today.

She picked it up and fanned it through, the ancient, cardboardy kind of smell reminding her of the old pony books from the fifties her mum used to try and palm off on her, before she gave up and took them to the Salvos. She leaned back and let the book fall open on her lap:

Ill met by moonlight, proud Titania.

Oberon, king of the fairies. Speaking to Titania, his queen; she knew that much. Having a domestic:

. . . Fairies,
skip hence; [cried Titania.]
I have forsworn his bed and company.

The word 'bed' was a bit of a shock, she thought. You just didn't think of fairies having sex. Somehow images of warm beds and rumpled sheets didn't go with the tippy toes and fairy wings of childhood. It was *Snugglepot and Cuddlepie*, not *The Secret Life of Us* or *Sex and the City*. And Titania and Oberon were really getting stroppy, each accusing the other of being unfaithful. Words and phrases seemed to jump out with a strange life of their own: 'amorous . . . Your buskin'd mistress and your warrior love . . . ravished . . . lead him through the glimmering night . . .'

Glimmering . . . Seph leaned back in her chair, staring at the word. A lovely sound – it made her think of zinging cicadas, gentle gusts of laughter and candles glowing through the dark.

She associated nights like that with their old house, in a proper, tree-filled suburb, where they'd lived before her father left. It had been a 'glimmering night' two years ago when her dad, Nick, had announced that he was moving out. With Lisa. A glimmering, glittering night filled with soft breezes off the harbour and the quiet murmur of her parents' voices wafting up from the garden. Suddenly there'd been a sharp cry, and the sound of a chair falling backwards. And those strange, strangled tones quickly turning to shouts . . .

Sometimes in the past when she'd heard them quarrelling, she'd walk into the room and they'd be forced to stop. This time, even though she couldn't actually hear the words, the stark shock and anger in her mother's voice had sent her creeping into Hedy's room, out of earshot, to curl up tight against her little sister's sleeping warmth.

$16x^2 - 8x + 6 = 0$

Perhaps, Seph thought now, she'd log in, just for a second, to see if anyone else was having trouble with their homework. But what if Tom had gone to Pia's place and they'd ended up doing their homework together? She wouldn't want to know about that.

And then the phone rang. It'd be Susan, she thought, calling from the conference dinner to check on them. Phoning in on the extra, separate line in her bedroom – the one she tried to keep free for her own calls. However, when Seph walked out into the passage she realised that it was the study phone, not Susan's, ringing.

'Hedy,' she called down the stairs, 'turn that TV off right now and get to bed!'

But Hedy wasn't downstairs, glued to *South Park*. She was there in the study, logged into what, as Seph picked up the phone, looked suspiciously like a chat room.

'Hi, Mum,' said Seph, trying to make her voice sound breezy and in control. She turned to Hedy, making furious go-to-bed gestures. Susan paid her an allowance to babysit Hedy on nights like this.

But it was Pia – bloody Pia – who chirped: 'It's me. Where are you? Log in, why don't you – we're having a great ol' rave!'

'Who's "we"?' Seph asked after a moment, gripping the receiver tightly.

Pia and Tom, their two heads bent over Pia's screen, chatting to everyone else? Or maybe Pia and Tom, having a private chat . . .

'Oh, Pak, and Wez, but he had to go and finish his assignment, and . . . Annie.'

So, not Tom. And Pia's pause before 'Annie' was the

cue, she knew, for Seph to laugh and say something like 'Annie? That wouldn't be Annie the half-sister of *Simon*, by any chance?'

And Seph felt hugely relieved, because obviously Pia was still interested in Simon, and not at all, she hoped, in Tom.

And then she felt angry again. Why on earth had Pia led Tom on like that?

Because Pia couldn't help herself, that was why. So Seph just said, 'Hmmph!'

'Seph, I found out all *sorts* of info, in a subtle kind of way of course.'

'Of course.'

Sometimes she really hated Pia.

'He's in Year 12, like Wez said. And guess what?' Pia added, her voice rising several decibels. 'He's probably going to be picked for the schools debating team – for the whole state!'

'Wow.'

'Se-eph . . .'

'No, I mean wow, P, that's great.'

'Wouldn't it be wonderful if he asked me out? Like . . .' (huge sigh down the line) 'as if he *would* or anything, but wouldn't it be wonderful?'

'Why don't you ask *him* out?' said Seph. 'You can get his number from Annie.'

'As if!' came Pia's squawk. 'I don't want to look desperate!'

Seph stared bleakly at Hedy's chat room. Someone called Chipper was announcing that he or she was nine and had two cats and a hamster called Fudge.

She shifted the receiver to her other ear and sighed.

'He'll ring. You know he will, Pia.'

It was inevitable; always a case of bees and the old honeypot with boys and Pia. And it wasn't just her looks; there was something else about her. Something, Seph had decided, that she, Seph, would never have. If she did have it then Tom wouldn't even have noticed Pia.

Seph had had a dream the other night in which she was a grey stone in the middle of the desert. And all around her beautiful, painted balloons were lifting off and floating away.

'Oh, d'you think so? Anyway, he's probably going out with someone, probably lots of girls – in his own year. Not some kid in Year 10.'

Seph became aware that Hedy had flicked to another, less suitable room; groova796chick was chatting to BARF45boy and smackohed320.

'Don't be stupid,' she said angrily, poking Hedy in the shoulder and pointing hard in the direction of the door. Pia's obvious fishing for compliments was just about the last straw.

On the other end, silence.

'Sorry,' said Seph, 'but I'm just trying to get *Hedy* to go to bed!' She put her hand over the mouthpiece. 'I'll tell Mum, and you won't get any pocket money.'

Hedy slowly started to quit the chat room.

'Just leave it,' Seph cried, 'and go!'

Then she removed her hand and asked: 'Did you end up catching the bus home with Tom tonight?' Trying to make it sound like idle chat, but she could hear it coming out all wobbly. She eased herself into the computer chair, still warm from Hedy.

'Yeah . . . he's quite cute, in a dopey kind of way.'

Seph's heart began to pound; horrible images flashed through her brain.

'Not my type, though,' added Pia airily.

Seph gave a short laugh. Small comfort, she thought bitterly. She took a deep breath; her hand felt all sweaty on the phone.

'Well, he certainly seems to like *you*.'

'Tom?' But Pia didn't sound particularly surprised. 'Nah,' she said dismissively. 'Nah, not Tom.'

Seph couldn't help herself. 'Bet he asked you out or something!'

As soon as she'd blurted it out, she could've kicked herself.

There was a small, frightening pause on the other end. 'No, he didn't,' said Pia finally, 'as a matter of fact.'

Then: 'Why? Why would *you* be so interested all of a sudden?'

'I'm *not*.'

Her heart was racing. Way too much emphasis, Seph, way.

Another silence.

'I think you a-are . . .'

The moment Seph let herself smile, she knew she was lost. It was almost as though Pia could see her face.

'Come on, Persephone, 'fess. I've had a hunch – you like him a bit more than just as a friend, don't you?'

'*Not*!' But Seph was starting to giggle. 'I hardly know him,' she spluttered indignantly. She took a big choking breath. 'I don't like him like *that*, honestly!'

But she could see Pia on the other end, head tilted, grinning her head off.

Oh, to hell with it.

'Well, if you tell *anyone*, Pia Halliday, I'll murder you!'

⟵⟶

And now it was out Seph felt really sick. Because of course Pia *would* end up telling. In her chatty, I'm-your-best-friend kind of way she just wouldn't be able to not tell. Maybe not Tom himself (she hoped!) but certainly Annie, next time she saw her.

Seph pictured the two of them, hanging out in Annie's room, going through a stack of CDs. Pia would be stretched out sideways on the bed, head in hand; Annie sitting on the floor, leaning back against her scratched old desk.

'Tom's a funny thing, isn't he?' Pia might suddenly remark, smiling a little and picking at the sheet.

Annie, arms on knees, Ani Difranco's voice washing over her like a wave, would smile absently and nod. Then she'd cock her head sideways. 'Why?'

Pia'd shrug and give a little laugh, her finger tracing a trail through poly-cotton stars. 'Oh, I dunno. He just seems a little lost, that's all . . .'

Trailing off, waiting for Annie to say something. (Like, that Annie happened to know that Tom actually had the hots for Pia?) But if Annie just shrugged and said something like 'maybe' or 'you reckon?', Pia would come right out with it: 'You know, for god's sake don't tell anyone I told you, but Seph really *likes* him.'

And now Seph lay in bed, hardly able to breathe. She turned her head towards her desk and stared across at the framed photo, barely still upright among the shadowy clutter of books and papers and clothes. Taken in the last week of the holidays, at Lantern Bay; all of them (except Pak, who was home in Bangkok) sitting on the beach, clowning for the camera. She'd had to keep hopping about while she was taking it, the sand was so hot.

'Smile!' she'd cried, and Tom, right in the middle, face in his hands, had seemed to give her a special, private grin.

And now Seph had to restrain herself from switching on the light and going over and picking up the photo. She'd stared at it so many times in the past couple of weeks it was a wonder there wasn't a hole worn in it. His greenish eyes slitty in the sun, his brown, salt-dried hair . . .

Her mother was moving about in the bathroom next door. Water ran, a pipe clanged.

That was the day he'd come up with Annie, Seph remembered, on the train. Even though he'd been Annie's neighbour forever, Seph hadn't seen him (or at least taken any notice of him) since primary school. Tom, of course, had been a year ahead of her, but they'd been in a composite class together at one stage.

'Brought a friend,' Annie'd announced, dumping her bag and passing Wez another bag containing Coke and munchies. She jerked her head over her shoulder.

'You remember Tom? He's going to Grammar this year, so you guys'd better be nice to him.'

Tom had stood just behind Annie in the doorway, towel over his shoulder, smiling, and Seph'd felt her heart suddenly lift. And when Annie'd got to Seph in the intros, he'd just grinned at her and said, 'Hey, Seph – long time. Year 5/6, wasn't it? Mrs Jackson's class?'

'Oh . . .' Seph could feel her face starting to get warm, '. . . wasn't it Mr Christopherson?' Then swallowed, feeling a total dork.

Wez laughed. 'Mrs Jackson? Mr Christopherson? Which?', and Pia cried, 'Get it *right*, for heaven's sake!'

But Tom had ignored them, kept looking at Seph.

'Your hair was always getting caught in the zipper of your uniform,' he said. 'I used to sit behind you, a couple of seats back.'

'Oh,' said Seph again. 'W-was it?' But she remembered, instantly; almost had to stop herself touching the back of her neck. That fierce tug of her snagged ponytail, and the giggling as she and . . . Rebecca? Yes, Rebecca Donato it was, in the next seat, who used to try and help her untangle it. Her mum had never got around to replacing the zipper.

She'd forgotten all that, completely.

'To-om,' said Annie, 'you're embarrassing the poor girl!'

By now Seph's face was beginning to throb.

'Yeah, take a look at her,' chuckled Wez. He reached across and laid the back of his hand on Seph's cheek, then whipped it away. 'Whoo!' he cried, shaking his hand. 'Red hot!'

And Seph just stood there, making a face at bloody Wez, wanting to sink through the floor. Feeling Tom's eyes on her still.

For the rest of that day Seph'd felt as though her head was not quite connected to her body, as though she had an invisible antenna tuned in to his whereabouts. Before going down to the beach they'd all sat around the table out on the balcony drinking coffee. She was talking to Wez's mum but was keeping one ear cocked to the other end, where he was perched on a stool between Wez and Annie. He wasn't saying much. Was he . . . perhaps looking at her occasionally, or had that brief bit of memory-lane stuff been it? She'd acted like a total dill.

She could hear her own voice mechanically answering Mrs Tupper's questions about electives and sport. And then Wez's laughter had given her an excuse to turn around, she'd sneaked a look, and – zap!

He was looking at her too.

She'd kind of half smiled at him and turned back to Wez's mum.

And when they'd all gone down for a swim he'd been just behind, with Wez, but then he'd caught up and chucked his towel down next to hers on the beach.

The lights of a car moving down the narrow street outside Seph's bedroom washed across her walls and ceiling as the swirl and glitter of the surf that day flooded her brain and made her roll onto her stomach and remember the warmth of the sand beneath her towel. She and Tom had lain there, propped on their elbows, hair dripping, gradually turning away from all the joking and blockout-tossing and towel-flicking, to one another.

Their hands ceaselessly smoothing curves in the sand, they'd started to talk. The sun bit unnoticed into the backs of their legs; they laid their faces sideways on their towels and kept talking, their eyes partly closed, their lips barely framing the words.

'Coming in again, guys?'

Seph jerked and twisted around, eyes opening wide. It was Pia standing there, casting a shadow right along Seph. Her neck was long and slender above her bikini top, the sun kissing her topknotted hair. Laugh-a-minute best friend, stealer of boys she didn't even want.

But he hadn't seemed to take much notice of Pia that day.

Seph lay there, rigid, sweaty, staring at the ceiling. She closed her eyes, then immediately opened them again. Looked at her clock.

12.45. Shit. And she had a French test in the morning.

She switched on her light and took a few gulps of water from her bedside glass, irritably kicking the sheet off her feet. So *hot*. She could hardly breathe it was so airless. The afternoon southerlies hadn't arrived; not a whisper of breeze seemed to be penetrating the close-packed streets of their inner city neighbourhood. Through the open window next to her bed she could almost feel the heat still radiating off the terrace houses opposite. And the little fan clipped to her bookcase hardly seemed to be making a dent in the air.

Finally she reached for her book, one of Susan's

murders-and-morgues thrillers and it was getting really scary.

Too scary. She put it down again; she'd never get to sleep.

But she knew what *would* send her off . . .

She sighed, rolled out of bed and padded across the rug, grabbing the play. She might as well, especially since she remembered hearing somewhere that whatever you read just before you went to sleep really sank in. If she got to sleep at all, that is.

She propped herself up, flicked determinedly to Act I.

Scene 1: Theseus the Duke, and then Egeus and his daughter Hermia come in with Lysander and Demetrius, her two suitors. Yeah, she remembered all this – Hermia was supposed to be marrying Demetrius, who was in love with her, but she and Lysander had fallen for one another instead. Egeus and Demetrius were really pissed about it.

Hermia was given a range of options. She could obey her father and marry Demetrius, become a nun, or be executed! What kind of a vile old bastard of a father was Egeus to agree to such a choice?

Seph thought of her own father in the same situation and smiled wryly. 'Sorry, old mate,' he would have said, his glasses glinting as he scratched his head and apologetically patted Demetrius on the back. 'She seems to've changed her mind.'

After all, he would hardly have been able to come over all self-righteous, seeing he'd done a bunk himself.

Concentrate, Persephone, concentrate.

The others exited, leaving the lovebirds alone together to bemoan their fate in all those high-fallutin' words. That's what got to her – if they were really crazy about one another, she thought, they'd be rushing into each other's arms, not standing there spouting poetry.

But then she wondered if Shakespeare meant them to be pashing, in between all the words. She remembered back to the year before, when Year 9 had been taken to see a schools performance of *As You Like It*, staged by a professional theatre company. The stage lovers had been all over one another. In one scene a jester had practically made love to a country wench right there on stage. Some of the boys from the school behind them had stamped and whistled and carried on so badly that the actors'd had to stop the performance and ask them to shut up. Even though she didn't know any of the boys from bars of soap, Seph'd felt totally mortified.

And, of course, there was all that passion in the movie version of *Romeo and Juliet* . . .

Seph went over the lines again, imagining herself as the director:

Lysander: [taking Hermia in his arms] *How now, my love?* [Stroking her cheek] *Why is your cheek so pale?*
How chance the roses there do fade so fast?
Hermia: [wiping her eyes] *Belike for want of rain, which I could well*
Beteem them from the tempest of my eyes.
Lysander: [kissing away the tears] *Ay me . . .*

Etcetera.

With actions put in, the words started to come to life. And then Hermia and Lysander were talking and half joking about true love and everything that can go wrong with it, and Lysander said:

The jaws of darkness do devour [love] *up,*
So quick bright things come to confusion.

Quick bright things come to confusion. How completely apt. Seph slapped savagely at a mozzie whining around her ear. She couldn't have put it better herself. That day, so dazzlingly bright, happiness had just come so completely and suddenly, out of the blue. His hand playing 'shark' with her ankle underwater, his eyes laughing into hers when his head popped out of the surf. That chat on the sand, the trip home in the car that evening, his arm along the back of the seat behind her, his bare leg, a slightly darker shade of gold brushing hers every now and again. The tyres of Mrs Tupper's Pajero singing down the freeway.

And even though they'd both been joining in all the talk and laughter, it'd seemed to Seph that each little comment or joke she or Tom made had been really meant for the other.

But what if she'd just imagined the whole thing?

What if it had been all on her side? What if it had been quite plain to him and everyone else what a fool she was making of herself, showing how much she liked him, throwing herself at him . . .

She lay there motionless, her head so hot on the

pillow. For the hundredth time she tried to conjure up that first smile of his, his expression when their eyes had met.

Come to confusion.

But all she could hear and see were the jokes and laughter of the others, and the roar and greenish thump of the waves.

CHAPTER 3

Next morning the phone rang. It was her father.
'Seph! How are you, darling?'

'Hi, Dad.' Seph swallowed a mouthful of toast.
'Want Mum?'

She heard him sigh; his big leather chair creaked.
He would have been at work, she knew, for a couple
of hours already. 'Is she there?' he asked, finally.

'In the shower, I think.' She glanced across the room
to where Hedy, hair unbrushed, feet bare, was sitting
on the sofa, engrossed in Susan's laptop. 'Hedy, Mum
still in the shower?'

The rumpled head remained bent over the screen,
motionless.

'*Hedy*!'

'Mmm . . .'

'Is Mum —'

But the round face had suddenly shot up. 'That
Dad?'

'Yep.'

Hedy tossed the computer to one side and hurtled across the family room. 'Dad!' she cried, grabbing at the receiver. 'Lemme speak to him!'

Seph frowned and handed it over, pretending not to hear her father's hurried 'Seph?' She took a final swig of tea, stacked her mug and plate in the dishwasher and headed for her room. The familiar Hedy-speak, tumbling over itself into the phone, followed her up the stairs: '. . . playing my violin at the Year 5 concert . . . Louisa's got the chicken pox . . . got two merit cards last week', and: 'Can I come to your place this weekend?'

'Seph?' her mum called from her bedroom. 'Is that your father on the phone?'

'Mu-um,' Hedy yelled simultaneously, 'it's Dad!'

Loud sigh from Susan. 'What does he want?' Seph heard her call. Then: 'Tell him I'm —'

Another sigh, even louder; she picked up the extension.

'What is it, Nick? Look, I know you're probably on your third espresso by now — hang up, please, Hedy — but at the moment I'm trying to get two children off to school, in case you've forgotten what that's like.'

Mechanically, Seph started stuffing books into her backpack. The familiar school bag smell of stale lunches and pencil sharpenings rose into her nostrils. As if we didn't get our own breakfasts and write out our own canteen orders, she thought dully. It's not as though we're babies.

And speaking of babies, Seph wondered what the

newspapers and legal bigwigs would say if they could hear her 'high profile' parents going hammer and tongs at one another like this. 'Susan Jarratt', a headline had trumpeted a couple of weeks ago, 'Voice of Reason in the Trade Union Scrum'. Underneath there'd been a photo of Susan, followed by a couple of her staff, hurrying into a meeting with some government minister or other. Seph hadn't bothered to read the article. And her father, a barrister, was almost as prominent. 'Counsel for BHP, Nicholas Harkness, SC, was yesterday quoted as saying . . .'

And here they were, bickering and sniping at one another like a couple of three year olds in a sandpit.

She heard her mother's heels tap across the polished floor; the door of the built-in slid back with a thump.

'It just might not be convenient, that's all,' Susan said crisply. 'I'll have to check what we've got on.'

Pause. Click, click, click went the hangers as she flicked briskly through her row of jackets. Then: 'I'm aware of that, strangely enough.' Sarcasm positively dripping. 'So perhaps you'd care to display some fatherly behaviour –'

Interjection from Nick; snort from Susan.

'*Like*, taking her to get some new gym shoes, for example! That's what she really needs. I don't see why it's always me who has to . . .'

On and on, the same old carry-on. Seph grabbed her maths textbook, accidentally knocking over the Lantern Bay photo. She picked it up, trying not to look at the face right in the middle. Everybody smiling so happily . . .

There was a very similar photo in one of the old albums, of her parents, long before they were married, on the beach with a group of their uni friends. Young Nick, his hair thick and shoulder-length, with disgusting fluffy sideburns growing down his face, had his arm around a slim, incredibly youthful-looking Susan. Their heads were tilted towards one another; her gaze was caught looking sideways at him, adoring.

'Seph's got her own life to lead,' Susan was shouting. 'You can't expect her to drop whatever it is she's got organised just because you suddenly want to see her.'

Pause, another loud sigh. 'All right, just a minute. Seph,' she called wearily, 'd'you want to go to your father's place on Sunday – with Hedy?'

'Oh . . .'

And all at once Seph felt horribly guilty, because the answer was no, she didn't. It'd probably be raining and there'd be nothing to do at his apartment except sit around and watch TV. Lisa would retire to the study to work, and Nick'd suggest the three of them go to a movie. But of course it woud have to be PG rated, for Hedy.

She pictured her father leaning forward over the phone, a slight, hopeful smile on his face, and felt another pang. Then she envisaged the complete waste of a Sunday. Bugger him, she thought, walking across her room. It was his fault for taking off in the first place.

She poked her head around her mother's door. 'Tell him sorry,' she said, 'but I've got a ton of homework to do on Sunday. Sorree,' she called, smiling apologetically in the direction of the receiver.

Her mother whirled triumphantly round to the window, the morning sun glinting on her auburn hair. 'You see, Nick. You can't expect them to be at your beck and call when you're not even . . .'

Round 256 to Susan, thought Seph wearily, going back to her room. She looked around for whatever else she needed, spied *A Midsummer Night's Dream* lying face down on the floor beside her bed. She didn't remember getting very far with it the night before.

She bent down and picked it up, glancing at the page. Act II Scene 1 – that furious blow-up between Titania and Oberon.

Seph sighed, stuffed the battered volume into her bag, and went to clean her teeth.

———⊃

'Now, "Love and Unreality in *A Midsummer's Night Dream*".'

Mrs Ahern stroked a stick of chalk back and forth along her upper lip. As a result of this habit, Seph noticed, Mrs A always seemed to have a faint white moustache.

Then she became aware that Mrs Ahern was frowning at her.

'. . . not at *all* happy with some of these essays.' She tapped the pile of papers on the desk beside her and frowned even harder.

Seph clasped her hands in front of her on the desk and bit her lip. It really had been dumb to hand in such a pathetic effort for their first assignment.

'I expect a lot more from girls in this class. I know you're perfectly capable of it.'

No more chat rooms during homework time, Seph told herself sternly. Think perfect uni entrance score, Seph, think cosmology course. Think Tom sighing sadly when he hears you're off to New York, invited by some handsome young astrophysicist to address a seminar . . . But then, right at the departure gate when you're about to go through customs, you'd turn around and there he'd be, thumbs hooked in his pants, smiling that slow smile of his. We'd look into one another's eyes and he'd say –

'Persephone Harkness, if you don't start paying attention this minute, I'll make you do that whole essay again. Yours was absolutely the worst. I don't know how that good little student I remember from Year 7 could have produced such rubbish!'

Seph's face burned; her heart thumped. That 'good little student' from Year 7 almost seemed like another person now, she thought. A clear-skinned, energetic twelve year old who used to enjoy discussing her essay topics with her father. He was around in those days.

Mrs Ahern picked up her copy of *A Midsummer Night's Dream* from the desk. 'Now, everybody turn to page nineteen. The end of Act I Scene 1. Everyone's left the stage except Helena – the bit where she's bemoaning the fact that Demetrius loves Hermia now, and not her. Melissa, could you read her speech to us, please?'

The class started flipping through their books.

Melissa began reading Helena's speech in her exaggeratedly rounded, 'I go to speech and drama class' voice:

How happy some o'er other some can be!
Through Athens I am thought as fair as she.
But what of that? Demetrius thinks not so . . .

As fair as she . . .

Seph glanced across to where Pia was leaning forward on her elbows over her book. A shaft of morning sun slanted in through the windows, bathing her skin and hair with gold.

It's not the same in our case, she thought. Pia's certainly prettier than me – anyone can see that. And yet . . .

Seph tried to imagine Pia with all that beautiful hair cut off and pimples dotted about her peachy complexion. After all, since Seph's sudden growth spurt the previous year, she was actually a bit taller than Pia, and about the same shape.

Pia yawned and massaged the back of her neck with her fingers; the fall of golden hair bobbed thickly up and down her back. No, thought Seph bitterly, if you shaved her head and dressed her in a plastic bag, she'd still be gorgeous. No wonder Tom had fallen for her; he'd be blind not to.

'Love looks not with the eyes, but with the mind,' Melissa declaimed, book held aloft. 'And therefore is winged Cupid painted blind.'

Blind? What does that mean, she wondered. If Tom were blind, would he still fall for Pia's sex appeal, that special sparky something Seph knew she herself just didn't have? Or did it mean that he was blind to Pia's annoying side, her flirtiness and stupid carry-on?

Pia suddenly looked across and caught Seph's gaze, rolling her eyes exaggeratedly in Melissa's direction. They grinned and started to giggle, Seph biting her lip very hard for fear of attracting Mrs A's attention. And Seph felt a rush of affection for her friend, and shame at her own jealousy. It wasn't Pia's fault she was born with a double dose of boy appeal.

Seph forced herself to look down at the page again. Concentrate, Persephone. She just knew Mrs A was going to ask her a question, any second. And sure enough, as soon as Melissa had sat down again, the teacher smiled at her.

'Seph, could you comment on the use of metaphor in lines two forty-two to five, please?'

Seph dived for the relevant section, her heart sinking. But as soon as she started to read, she relaxed. No probs with these lines :

For ere Demetrius looked on Hermia's eyne
He hailed down oaths that he was only mine,
And when this hail some heat from Hermia felt,
Soon he dissolv'd, and showers of oaths did melt.

Seph looked up at Mrs Ahern. 'Demetrius'd sworn that he only loved Helena,' she said, 'but he forgot it all the moment Hermia started paying him some attention?'

The lines were so relevant to her own situation it was unreal.

Mrs A tapped at her lip. 'Metaphor, Seph, I'm asking about Shakespeare's use of poetic *language*. The *meaning* is pretty clear.'

Seph looked down at the page again, chewing at her thumb. But even this wasn't hard. She'd never been a poetry freak, but these lines were somehow spot-on. She cleared her throat.

'She's saying Demetrius is like a kind of god, who sends down promises which are like hail,' she said slowly, her finger running along the lines. 'And Hermia is kind of like the sun. She melts the promises of love that he's made to Helena.'

Tom a god and Pia the bloody sun – that'd be right. Except Tom had never promised Seph anything.

'Thank you, Seph, very good.' Mrs Ahern hoisted herself backwards up onto her desk and sat there, feet swinging. The stick of chalk went scraping back and forth across her mouth like some kind of strange windscreen wiper.

'Shakespeare is invoking wild elements of the weather. It all helps to build up his vision *of* –'

Mrs A's eyebrows shot up; the chalk was momentarily still. There was silence; not one hand went up.

'Of,' she continued, 'the forces of love being *un*predictable – almost completely beyond our control.'

Seph picked up her pen and started inking a tiny black square into her book.

You can say that again, she thought bitterly. You can sure say that again.

⌒⌒

The study, 9.15 pm.

Seph was on the Net again, but this time doing proper work; research for her Australian History project. Even Susan, who'd gone out again after dinner to her bookclub would've approved.

Frowning, she scrolled down the list. A search for the topic 'racism and the white Australia policy' had produced a whole mass of stuff. Seph quite liked history, but this was all too much.

Everything was so quiet. The only sound was the faint whirr of the computer. The shelves of books above and around her stared down, silently accusing.

Australia's identity crisis . . . The policy of exclusion . . . Seph sighed, her mouse clicks becoming more random. She wondered if Pia had started her project yet, and how she was going.

Perhaps if she had a quick, *very* quick dive into chat, just to see if Pia was there, she could ask her. And if Pia wasn't there, she'd get out again, straight away. No arguments, Persephone. Not even if –

She zipped to 'Favourites'; whipped into 'Chat'. Up it came: Welcome sefi_15. Her eyes automatically travelled down to the 'Friends in Chat' square and –

Tom wasn't there. Just annidreama, tupper_wez and piachicki, no doubt raving on about nothing, as usual. Seph felt a stab of disappointment, wondered if she could even be bothered going in . . .

But anything had to be better than the White Australia Policy, so she highlighted 'piachicki' and clicked on 'Go to Friend' and there they were, rabbiting on as usual:

```
tupper_wez <how could u go if you were alreddy
gone?>
piachicki <hey evry1 guess WOT??>
```

Seph mentally groaned – fancy her coming in on
Pia's hot topic! She'd already had half an hour of it
on the phone the previous night. And half of lunchtime that day as well.

```
tupper_wez <sumtimes i wonder>
annidreama <wot?>
sefi_15 joined the room
sefi_15 <yawn>
sefi_15 <surprise surprise, he's rung her up>
tupper_wez <hey sefi>
annidreama <who's rung her?>
tupper_wez <hows things??>
piachicki <your brother actually>
annidreama <shock horror>
annidreama <god, p, I thought you had more taste!>
annidreama <yeah, tom said something about him
turning up at cappos>
```

Seph leant forward in her seat. Why would
Tom have especially mentioned it, unless he was
jealous?

She bit her lip and frowned at the offending line.

Suddenly she became aware of something – someone
– standing in the shadows behind her. She screamed
and whirled around.

But it was only Hedy, standing there in her nightie.

'Omigod, Hed, you scared me!' cried Seph, clutching at her heart.

Hedy, her face framed by wisps of red-gold hair, folded her arms and rubbed at her eye with one finger.

'I can't get to sleep,' she said. 'Can I stand here, just for a while?'

'No – it's very late!'

Hedy's gaze wandered past Seph's shoulder to the screen. Seph moved slightly to block her sister's view.

'You go straight back to bed!'

Hedy yawned, enormously. 'Will you come and pat me?'

Seph snorted. 'Oh for goodness *sake*, Hedy, you're much too old for that!'

Patting was a legacy from Hedy's pre-school days when the teachers had 'patted' some of the kids to sleep at their afternoon nap time. It vaguely bothered Seph that her sister, at the age of ten, still seemed to need this ritual from time to time. Although as Susan had pointed out, it beat thumb-sucking any day.

Now Hedy suddenly launched forward and wrapped herself around Seph's neck. Seph's face was squashed hard against Hedy's warm cheek.

'I'll tell Mu-um,' Hedy sang, 'that you've been chatting instead of doing your home-work!' She leant forward, peering intently at the screen. 'Piachicki . . . that's Pia, isn't it? Who's Tupper Wez?'

'*He-dy*!' Seph furiously tried to disentangle Hedy's arms, but they were suckered on tighter than an octopus's, practically choking her.

45

'Hey,' grinned Hedy. Her grip tightened. 'Is *Tom* here?'

'Now *look* –' Alarmed, Seph made one last mighty effort to escape, but collapsed into giggles instead.

'Just go!' she gasped, twisting around and trying to tickle Hedy in the ribs.

But Hedy was unrelenting. 'Pat?' she shrieked, arching her body backwards. 'If I let go, will you promise to pat me to sleep?'

'All right, I promise!'

'Really?'

'*Yes* – now let go!'

Hedy cautiously loosened her grip.

'Whew. *Thank* you.' Seph fanned exaggeratedly at her brow with both hands. It was hot enough without Hedy climbing all over her. She leant forward and typed <brb>, then clicked 'temporarily left room'.

'Now, go and get into *bed*!'

'Mum's bed,' said Hedy, bumping against the chair. 'I'm gunna sleep in Mum's bed tonight.'

'Dunno what Mum's going to say about that.' Ever since Nick had left Hedy was forever wanting to sleep in her mother's room, despite Susan's efforts to discourage it.

Hedy grabbed Seph's hand and started pulling her up. 'Come on, Seph.'

<dont be long sefi baby!> came tupper_wez's plea across the screen, but Seph was already halfway out the door.

Later, back again:

sefi_15 <i really gotta GO and do this bloody project>
piachicki <so - who's he been going out with>
sefi_15 <anyone know anything about the white aust policy????>
piachicki <anyone id know?>
piachicki <& dont u dare tell him ive been asking all these questions!>
tupper_wez <it's a policy of changing Cs to As before your olds see your report>
annidreama <as if - i hardly ever see him these days>
annidreama <i wouldnt have a clue who hes been taking out>
sefi_15 <ha HA - i said white australia, not white out>
sefi_15 <im wasting my time on you lot>
tupper_wez <same thing>
sefi_15 <i shld be engaged in intellectual pursuits>
piachicki <dont go, seph>
annidreama <where r the others tonite??>
piachicki <i havent even started my project yet>

Seph was just about to click 'Exit' when the latest entry froze her finger on the mouse:

grEMLin joined the room

She leant forward, frowning, as the unfamiliar name started slowly moving up the screen amongst the chat.

piachicki <u kno seph, melissa wos asking about coming in here, but i wos vague>
piachicki <we dont want just anyone in here>
tupper_wez <what the - gremlin - who r u???>
annidreama <gremlin?>
tupper_wez <i bet - ok pak, or is it tom>
tupper_wez <which 1 of u has changed your name?>
sefi_15 <bet its pak>
annidreama <speak to us gremlin>
piachicki <hey - this is a PRIVATE chat room - members only>

Seph double-clicked on gremlin; clicked 'Profile'. But there was nothing. No email address, no hobbies, no likes and dislikes, not even whether gremlin was male or female. It was like a spirit from thin air. Or rather, thin cyberspace. Some kind of virus maybe?

And he or she was still there, silent, lurking in the room.

annidreama <hey - howd u get in here anyway?>
piachicki <gremlin - either say somefink or piss off>
tupper_wez <hey - i just ducked in next door 2 chek on pak>
tupper_wez <& hes not there>
tupper_wez <hes probly taken his laptop down to the library>

sefi_15 <so u can be the gremlin in peace eh pak?>
annidreama <HEY - ive just dialled toms number and its engaged>
annidreama <theyve only got 1 fone line>
piachicki <it could be tom>
sefi_15 <his mum or he could just be on the phone>
tupper_wez <nip next door & peek in his window why doncha annie>

Seph stared at the monitor; at grEMLin sitting there in the room list. Why would Tom or Pak be bothered to come in and sit there like that, under a different name?

And Seph suddenly felt a cold, creepy feeling, despite the warmth of the night.

She told herself not to be dumb. It would just be some nerd from Dayton, Ohio (or more likely Ipswich, Queensland, or Christchurch, New Zealand, given the different time zones) who somehow happened to have stumbled into their room. He mightn't even know he was in there – he was probably just quiet because he'd taken himself off to the bathroom mirror to squeeze a pimple, or to the kitchen to get a snack.

Still, even though she knew she was being crazy, Seph got up to go and check all the doors and windows. She crept downstairs, keeping to the edge of the stairwell, and padded along the shadowy hall to test the front door lock. She nearly tripped over something in the living room, but it was only Hedy's open violin case, left smack in the middle of the floor. The strings gleamed very faintly in the darkness.

She crossed back to the kitchen and decided to close the glass doors leading onto the balcony, despite the waft of air nudging next door's windchimes. The back courtyard lay one level below, but someone determined enough could surely climb up the thick ropes of trumpet vine hugging the corners of the house.

She even made a quick dash down the back stairs to the darkened rumpus room, even though she knew perfectly well that the bottom doors were locked.

She padded back up to the top floor. This is really stupid, she thought. The gremlin's on the Net, not out there in the street. Yet she still switched on several more lights, peered behind doors and in cupboards, and checked the window catches.

Last of all she poked her head around Susan's door. Hedy was lying sprawled across the bed in a tangle of sheet, her hair spread out in a reddish fan across the pillow. Seph could hear her breath going in and out.

Downstairs the fridge gave a shudder, then everything was deathly quiet again. Seph turned around and hurried back to the study.

To find grEMLin still there, still silent, despite all the attention.

piachicki <cmon pak?? - we know u wanted to open up the room>
tupper_wez <who cares - sit there if u want>
tupper_wez <we're not that interesting>
annidreama <funny way of opening it up>

Suddenly:

grEMLin <o but u r all interesting>

Silence. Seph leant forward, holding her breath.

piachicki <how the hell wld u know>
grEMLin <i kno all about u>

Another pause.

sefi_15 <spill then>
grEMLin <who u luv, sef, and pia too>

Seph's insides lurched crazily. *Don't*! she wanted to scream. That's enough!

tupper_wez <tell us!>
grEMLin <nah - yul just have to wait wont u, till next time>
piachicki <whaa - why???>
grEMLin <don worry, ill be back!>
grEMLin <bye for now>
grEMLin left the room

CHAPTER 4

'It must be Pak, or Tom,' said Pia the next morning, stuffing books from her bag into her locker. 'Else how would an outsider get into a private chat room?'

Seph stood on tiptoe and felt along the back of her top shelf for her French dictionary. 'Well, obviously all the gremlin would have to know,' she said slowly, her fingers encountering fluff, several gum wrappers, a hairclip, her other (broken) watch, and a lunchbox lid missing since the first day back, 'is one of our nicknames. If he typed it into the "search for friend" section, we'd come straight up if we were online.'

'Well I haven't used my nickname anywhere else,' said Pia. 'Or told it to anyone. I don't think . . .' She frowned. 'And he used our real names at the end.'

'Hey, guys,' said Melissa suddenly, from right behind.

Seph and Pia turned around.

'Oh hi, Melissa.'

As usual Melissa was all set, books cradled in her arms. Her cheeks were pink, her eyes bright, a velvet ribbon tied back the crinkly bush of her hair.

She looked at Seph. 'Ready? We've got that grammar test this morning, remember?'

'Thank God I dropped French,' said Pia. She hurried off to catch up with some other girls, giving a little wave back over her shoulder.

Seph forgot about the dictionary and tried for her exercise book instead. The locker area was emptying fast; a couple more doors clanged shut. Of course I'm not ready, she felt like shouting. What's it bloody look like?

Instead she just mumbled: 'You go ahead, Melissa. Save me a seat.'

After the previous night she was feeling a little edgy.

In the double English period they had to write a short piece on the character of Puck in the play.

Puck, that 'shrewd and knavish sprite', 'that merry wanderer of the night', who wrought so much havoc in the lives of the young lovers. Who, under the direction of Oberon, even made a fool of Titania, causing her to fall ridiculously in love with a country yokel disguised as a donkey. A mischievous hobgoblin, a gleeful elf . . .

A gremlin.

Seph pressed her fingers hard into her forehead.

who u luv, sef . . .

Shit a brick.

But perhaps he wouldn't come back again; perhaps last night had been a one-off, and he'd just been a random wanderer in cyberspace. 'I'll put a girdle round about the earth/In forty minutes', Puck told Oberon. What would Shakespeare think, Seph wondered, if he could see the cyber-gremlins of today, rounding the globe in less than a second?

She stared at the blank page, biting her pen. 'The Character of Puck' she wrote finally, across the top of the page. She frowned, inking in the word 'Puck' more boldly. Then slowly, without thinking, she doodled a circle right around the 'u' and the 'c' and added a stroke down the right hand side to make the two letters into one 'a'.

Pak.

How would Pak know who she loved? Had it been that obvious?

But oh god, what if the gremlin was Tom?

Susan padded across the family room in her stockinged feet and switched on the television; the opening strains of *The Bill* blared forth. 'Hedy,' she said, turning to settle herself into the sofa, glass of wine in hand, 'I've already told you – off to bed!'

Hedy, who'd been curled up extra quietly at the other end, folded her arms and scowled.

'Aaw . . . just another fifteen minutes? *Please*? I'm not tired yet!'

Sometimes Hedy was like a worn cassette, the same lines repeated every night, over and over.

'You can go to bed and read for a while,' said Susan, her eyes glued to the TV. 'That'll put you to sleep!' Police lights flashed across the screen; a hatchet-faced policewoman got out of a car. 'I've already kissed you goodnight,' Susan added irritably. 'Now *go*.'

'*Aaw* . . .'

Hedy started very slowly to climb out of the sofa, turning her head around to Seph.

'If someone *read* to me I'd get sleepy!'

'Don't look at me,' muttered Seph from behind the kitchen bench, where she was helping herself to the last of the hokey pokey icecream. 'I've got a ton of home-work.'

And maybe a visit from the dreaded gremlin . . .

Her sister grinned. 'A ton of chatting more li –'

'*Hedy*!' Seph glanced quickly across at her mother, who, fortunately, was already too engrossed in the affairs of the South London constabulary to have registered Hedy's remark. 'Anyway,' she added sternly, 'you're ten, not six! You don't *need* to be read to any more!'

'Please, darling,' cried Susan, patting Hedy's hand, 'let me watch this! It's the one thing I watch all week.'

Goodness knows why, thought Seph, looking back at the screen. An old man in a dressing gown shuffled down his front path, collected his milk bottle and said good morning to a couple of patrolling policepersons.

'Can I sleep in your bed?'

Policepersons smiled and moved on. Old man shuffled back.

'Yes!' cried Susan. 'Good *night*!'

Then the phone rang. Hedy scuttled to answer it.

'Hello?' Her face lit up. 'Oh hi, Dad!'

From the sofa, a groan.

'Yep,' Hedy grinned, 'yep!' She nodded vigorously, the phone cord bouncing up and down. 'Yep, that'd be great!

'Mum,' she called finally, holding out the receiver, 'it's Dad. About me coming over on the weekend.'

'Tell him I'll call him back later.' Susan curled deeper into the cushions and folded her arms, slopping red wine onto her silk top in the process.

'Oh shit, now look what I've done!' She plonked her glass down on the coffee table and hauled herself up. 'Give it to me,' she said loudly, holding out her hand for the receiver as she made for the sink. 'May as well get it over with.'

'Hello.' The cord was stretched to the max; she leant over to grab a sponge from the drainer. 'Yep.' She wet the sponge under the tap and dabbed at her blouse furiously, soaking herself in the process. One side of her bra started to show through, like magic ink.

'Yep.'

Suddenly she froze, mid-dab. 'Now listen to me. If you want Hedy you'll have to come and pick her up.'

Seph scraped carefully at some butterscotch bits on the inside of the icecream lid. Hedy tried sneaking back to the sofa.

'Hedy!' cried Susan. She didn't put her hand over the mouthpiece as she would've if she'd been talking to anyone else. 'Seph, put Hedy to bed. *Now*, please!'

Seph rolled her eyes, made for the sofa and intercepted Hedy mid-flop.

'It's a shocking time to ring, as a matter of fact.' Susan hurled the sponge at the sink. 'Bloody awful, Nick!'

'Come on, Hed.' Seph pulled her sister close to her, Hedy's soft hair brushing against her cheek. Suddenly her throat was choked with tears. She took a deep breath.

'Let's go and see what old Harry Potter's up to.'

Seph plonked herself, her bowl of melted icecream and her books down at the computer. And sat there, staring at the blank screen. Then she pushed the bowl away. Her head was starting to ache; she felt shivery and flu-ish.

Stuff them, she thought, stuff them all. Stuff Susan and Nick and Pia and Tom, and particularly stuff the bloody gremlin. Let him say what he likes; just ignore it all and get on with your history project.

She reached down and switched on the computer. Clicked onto the Net, typed in her password. Moved the cursor onto 'Search'. It was too early for chat yet anyway.

But perhaps, she thought, she'd better just check. The 'Friends in Chat' square was empty.

She slumped in her chair, her relief almost physical. But it was only a temporary reprieve. A stay of execution, not a pardon. She looked at her watch: 8.35. After nine was more the tune-in time.

Yul just have to wait . . . till next time . . .

For the hundredth time she wondered if the gremlin was only bluffing, didn't really know a thing. Or, better still, if he'd gone, zapped forever into cyberspace.

Could gremlins simply vanish?

Suddenly she thought of Puck, turning up again and again in different guises to torment his victims. Pretending to be a stool in order to topple a fat house-wife, or a neighing foal, to madden a lonely mare. Leading drunks to ruin, lovers to total humiliation.

Seph could feel her heart beating; the palms of her hands were beginning to sweat.

She reached slowly for the library book she'd borrowed that day, flicked through to the index and forced her gaze down the dreary columns to 'w'. *Wharf labourers . . . Wheat industry, White – White Australia Policy, 27–9, 45, 62–7,* etcetera. She opened the book to page 27.

By the end of page 28, she realised she hadn't a clue what she'd read. She picked up her pen and started hatching thick black lines across the top of her notebook page. 'The White Australia Policy', approximately 1000 words and due in the following Monday, and it felt as though she was slowly setting in concrete.

Perhaps she'd go back to the Net, and just check the room on the way . . .

And when she did she found piachicki and tupper_wez had suddenly materialised in the 'Friends' box. No grEMLin, but she couldn't tell from that. She certainly hadn't added *him* to 'Friends'.

Hardly daring to breathe, she clicked on 'piachicki'.

But there was only the two of them, hanging there:

piachicki <hope u guys are coming to the social on sat>

The social. Seph hadn't wanted to think about it. A combined Year 10/11/12 affair for three or four different schools, including theirs, Grammar and Annie's school, Hilldene.

piachicki <cos we r>

Seph frowned. Oh yeah? It's all right for you, Pia dearest. The famous Simon would be there, of course.

tupper_wez <hey, pak n me r boarders remember>
tupper_wez <we'r forced to go>
piachicki <hardship!>
sefi_15 joined the room
piachicki <annies coming>
piachicki <hey seph!>
piachicki <& wez, get tom to come too>

Seph froze, fury and fear mingling in equal parts. Don't you dare, Pia, don't you dare . . .
What on earth could've possessed her to blab to Pia, of all people?
But Pia just continued:

piachicki <so - no gremlin??>
tupper_wez <we musta scared him off - yaaah gremlin>
piachicki <good riddance>

tupper_wez <he wos probly just a 1-off nu-sance>
piachicki <hey sef, annie sez we can get ready at her place>
tupper_wez <pak swears it wasnt him>
piachicki <before the social>

Then:

grEMLin joined the room

Silence.

piachicki <omigod>
grEMLin <hello>

Another pause.

tupper_wez <ok pak or tom - fess up or we'll put you on ignore>
grEMLin <but i wos going to tell you all about yourselves>
piachicki <well tell then>
grEMLin <yuv got a new boyfriend, havnt u>
tupper_wez <duh - tell us something we dont know>
piachicki <yeah!!!!!>
annidreama joined the room
tupper_wez <wot about seph??>

Seph was gripping one hand in the other so tightly it was starting to go numb. No no, she shouted inwardly, *not about Seph . . .*

annidreama <all here again?>
annidreama <still up to your tricks, pak, or tom?>
tupper_wez <pak took hisself off to the library - SUSPICIOUS>

Yeah, thought Seph, staring at the screen, it's gotta be Pak . . .
But suddenly:

p_a_k joined the room

General commotion.

tupper_wez <pak my boy, yer innocent!>

So, it must be —

piachicki <tom>
annidreama <ok then>
piachicki <like . . . why??????>
annidreama <im ringing your number right now, tom>
annidreama <youd better not be engaged>

And so on and so forth. Pak sounded quite hurt that no-one had believed him.
And all the while grEMLin was looking on, silent.
Then Annie came back on:

annidreama <just as I thought - toms numbers busy>
piachicki <ah-ha! plot thickens>

```
tupper_wez <cmon grem-tom - give it up>
p_a_k <look out tom, annies comin to get ya>
annidreama <hell no, im in my jarmies>
annidreama <cant be bothered>
```

Why on earth would Tom be doing this, Seph wondered. She thought of the crinkles at the corner of Tom's eyes when he smiled, of his hands hanging loosely at his sides. Somehow the picture of him as the sly gremlin lurking in the corner just didn't seem to fit.

A square was popping up in one corner of the screen – for private chat.

From grEMLin to sefi_15

Seph's breath caught in her throat. She stared at the name. And then at the message beneath:

```
<hey sef, wanna chat with me - just the 2 of
us?>
```

CHAPTER 5

Seph sat there very still, heart pounding, the flood of hope almost choking her. Easy, Seph, she thought, easy. It probably wasn't even him. The twerp from Ipswich or the nerd from New Zealand, more like, leaning forward over his keyboard, smirking and picking his nose . . .

But why would a stranger choose her, out of the five of them?

Perhaps he *had* sent a message to each of them.

The cursor in the reply box was blinking insistently, and suddenly she was filled with panic. Reply, she told herself, for god's sake reply, before he gives up and closes off the box! But careful . . . So she typed:

sefi_15 <what about?>
grEMLin <about the 2 of us>

came the reply, straight back.

Seph thought she was going to have a heart attack.
Shivers, it must be him – mustn't it? She wanted to
laugh and cry, all at once, but she forced herself to lift
her hands and type:

```
sefi_15 <what about us?>
grEMLin <we both no, dont we?>
grEMLin <our secret>
```

Seph took a deep, shuddery breath.
Calm down, Seph, stay cool.
It was as though she was balancing on the edge of
a precipice, not knowing whether she was going to fall
or fly.
Finally:

```
sefi_15 <who R you??>
grEMLin <u know who i am>
```

Seph leant forward, fingers hovering, mind racing
uselessly like a wheel stuck in mud. What to reply? A
'no' or a '???' might seem like she's not even interested;
a 'yes' too keen.
And the cursor was flashing and flashing, demand-
ing . . .
'Maybe', she'd type a 'maybe'. But as her finger
moved to the 'm', here he was again:

```
grEMLin <see you very soon!!>
```

Very soon . . . Seph stared at the words.
The social. He must be talking about the social!

Suddenly:

'Se-eph.'

It was Susan, her feet padding up the stairs, nearly at the top. Seph grabbed the mouse and quickly clicked – out of gremlin, out of the others, out of chat altogether. Back to ghastly White Australia –

Just as her mother stuck her head around the door.

'Seph?'

Seph whirled around, her face burning. 'Mmm?'

'Before I forget, what's happening on the –' Susan broke off, staring at her daughter. 'You okay?' Her gaze reached around Seph to the screen. She frowned suspiciously. 'You look all flushed.'

'Oh . . .' Seph automatically put a hand to her forehead. She shrugged and tried to laugh. 'No, I'm okay.'

'Well anyway, I'm trying to get the weekend organised. What are you doing on –' She stopped again, took a few steps into the room. 'What *is* the matter, lovie? Have you seen a ghost or something?'

Yeah, thought Seph, through her confusion. A cyber-ghost . . .

'I'm *fine*,' she said, scowling and turning back to the screen. 'What d'you want to know?'

'Have you got anything planned for Saturday night?'

'Oh,' Seph stared blankly at the print, struggling to keep her voice casual, 'the social, I s'pose . . .'

6.30 pm Saturday, Annie's room. Annie, Pia and Seph were getting ready. Pia still was, anyway; the other two had more or less finished. Pia's preparations always seemed to go on forever.

Now she was crimping her hair. She held the wand firmly clamped to one side of her hair, scooping a large blob of salsa on a corn chip with the other. 'Hey, Annie,' she said, munching loudly over the strains of Killing Heidi, '*you* should try some crimping.' She held out the chips. 'It'd look cool.'

She'd already had a go on Seph.

Annie, sitting cross-legged on her bed, put a hand to her head in alarm. 'Me? No way. I'd look ridiculous!'

Her other hand was resting on her miniature fox terrier Bean, who, from her prime spot beside Annie, was keeping a close eye on the munchies.

'No you *wouldn't*!' Pia cried, still staring at herself.

'Yes I *would*! And anyway,' added Annie, taking the bowl and feeding Bean a couple of chips, 'two of you's enough.' She looked at Seph and grinned. 'Three of us'd look like a mob of sheep!'

'Baa! Baaa!' giggled Pia.

Seph craned in towards the mirror, suddenly panicked. Pia smiled back at her in the glass.

'Don't we look groo-vee?' said Pia, in a pseudo *Friends* kind of accent.

'*You* do,' said Seph, frowning. Somehow Pia's long golden crimps, even with only one side finished, looked perfect. By comparison her own attempt suddenly seemed just . . . try-hardish.

The room was filled with the odour of singeing. Pia

66

opened the wand and surveyed the end result with an air of professional satisfaction. She turned back to Annie, the appliance held aloft.

'It'd make you look –'

About six, thought Seph, glancing at Annie. As though she were dressed in patent leather shoes and her best Sunday school dress.

Annie was very small with braces on her teeth, her brown hair cut in a helmet-like, Joan of Arc style. Seph had never forgotten her own mortification the day Hedy, aged about six, had marched up to Annie and asked her if she was a boy. The expression on Annie's face . . .

Susan and Hedy had been dropping Seph off at the first day of a pony camp which Annie also happened to be attending. Because of her embarrassment at Hedy's lack of tact, Seph had been especially nice to Annie for the next few days. The two of them had become friends and remained so ever since, even though they'd always been at different schools.

'It'd make me look stupid!' Annie finished, picking up her pink pig cushion and hurling it at Pia. 'About as stupid as you are, Halliday!'

The cushion missed Pia and knocked over a glass of water on the dressing table. The puddle spread out towards Annie's precious collection of AC/DC memorabilia under the mirror.

Pia shrieked, Bean barked. But Annie leapt off the bed, grabbed a handful of tissues and stemmed the flow, at the same time whisking her most prized trophy, an ancient, grubby-looking school tie, out of harm's way.

'Angus's tie!' she croaked, inspecting it for water damage. She clasped it to her chest. 'Phew, that was close!'

'It could probably do with a wash,' said Pia. She looked at the rest of the motley collection of objects and wrinkled her nose. A broken guitar string, a charred cigarette packet, an autographed paper serviette and several faded ticket stubs were arranged in a kind of shrine in front of a couple of framed photos.

'Disgusting old relics!' said Pia, Seph adding: 'A health hazard, most probably.'

Annie absently tossed another chip to beady-eyed Bean before passing the bowl to Seph. 'Prob'ly,' she agreed cheerfully.

Ever since the time, at the age of twelve, that she'd gotten to hear *Highway to Hell* from her uncle's old record collection, Annie had been addicted to AC/DC. And more particularly to Angus Young, the guitarist, who at 157 centimetres tall was just about her size.

Actually, it was the seventies version of Angus she loved, not the Angus of now. It was a bad day for Annie when, having saved for and fronted up to a long-awaited AC/DC concert the year before, she discovered the shocking truth. Her idol was now in his forties – and even older than her father! The wild boy of Annie's dreams had morphed into an ancient old wrinkly.

'Well don't laugh at me then,' Annie's mother Cath had said, 'for liking Robert Redford or Harrison Ford – the way *they* were.'

Seph put down the chips – she certainly didn't feel

like eating – and was peering down in horror at something lurking behind the cigarette packet. Finally she took a deep breath, pinched it between her thumb and forefinger and gingerly picked it up.

Pia squealed and stepped backwards.

'Annie,' said Seph sadly, dangling the object out in front of her, 'don't tell me . . .'

Annie nodded solemnly.

'Yep,' she said quietly, 'Bon's. Scrounged from where he dropped it the day before he died.'

Seph and Pia stared in horror at the used tomato sauce bubble, its dried red tidemark still visible through the plastic.

Annie laughed and gave them both a little shove.

'No, dorks, I just cleaned out my uniform pockets!'

More shrieks and now it was Annie's turn to get pushed. She collapsed backwards onto the bed, narrowly missing Bean.

'Look out,' she yelled, 'you nearly made me squash Bean!' She put an arm around the little dog, fondling her ears. 'Sorry, bubba!'

Bean, her paws resting daintily over the edge of the bed, grinned at Annie forgivingly.

'Be hard to squash Bean,' said Pia. 'She's like a –'

'Little barrel,' said Seph, laughing. 'A barrel on legs, aren't you, Bean?'

'Beanie Bean,' sang Annie, putting her hands over Bean's ears, 'they're being rude about yooou.'

'Nah,' said Seph, bending down, 'we love ya, Bean.'

It was impossible to imagine Annie's house without the little dog around, her nails clicking across the kitchen tiles, her eyes round and bright above her dark muzzle.

Seph plonked herself down on the bed next to Annie, clasping her arms around her knees. Right there, through the open window, was the wall of Tom's house, dark bricks glowing warm in the evening light. She could see a window a bit further along, a small, bathroom-type one.

Was he in there now, getting ready for the social? She imagined him leaning into the mirror, towel wrapped around his waist . . . shaving?

Did guys of sixteen shave?

Pia was applying another coat of lipstick. She whirled around.

'How do I look?' She struck a Marilyn Monroe-ish pose, one hip pushed out, head flung back, fingertips brushing the nape of her neck. 'Reckon he'll *lahke* me?'

Seph and Annie looked at one another.

'Who?' asked Annie innocently.

Pia made a face. 'Who d'you think?'

Annie put a finger to her lips. 'Oh,' she said finally, 'you mean *Simon*?'

Eye-roll from Pia.

Annie sighed, wearily. 'Trust me, Pia. He'll like you.'

Seph stared at Pia, all glowy in her boob tube and tight skirt. And felt herself going cold and heavy, like a stone.

With Pia around, why would Tom even want to look at someone like her?

'Tom coming?' Annie's stepfather, Ian, picked up the car keys from the bench. 'Does he want a lift with us?'

Seph struggled to keep her face neutral, even though she'd been wondering the same thing ever since she'd arrived. She avoided looking at Pia.

'No,' said Annie, 'I think he said he was going there from a friend's place or something.'

Seph felt a stab of disappointment. But surely he'd show up, wouldn't he?

Annie glanced over at her mother, who was peeling raw prawns at the sink. 'Bye, Mum.'

Cath raised a cheerful, mucky hand. She and Ian, Seph thought wistfully, were always so warm and welcoming.

'Bye, girls.' Cath smiled at them. 'You look gorgeous!'

If only, thought Seph as they trooped after Ian through the laundry door to the garage. Her stomach was beginning to churn.

If only . . .

—)

'Names, girls?' The teacher at the entrance desk looked enquiringly at Seph and Pia; she already knew Annie. She had to shout over the noise of the milling crowds and the music bursting out into the foyer from the hall itself.

Seph and Pia gave up trying to yell and merely pointed out their names on their own school list. Then the three of them made their way through the throng to the double doors at the end, eyeing the crowd for familiar faces as they went.

Walking into the hall was like opening the door to a furnace: they were hit by a solid blast of noise and heat and light. Under the strobe the sea of kids seemed to jerk and flare like a scene from a not-so-silent movie; hands, torsos and faces caught in hundreds of flickering, disembodied freeze-frames. Techno blasted; the lights of the disco booth blinked jarringly out of time with the strobe. And from their framed positions high among the honour rolls and dusty banners, the faces of past principals beamed down their split-second flashes of disapproval, like weird and ghostly dummies in a sideshow.

The three girls stood there, momentarily frozen.

'Come on,' shouted Annie at last, 'let's see if we can find –'

'*Hey* –'

Melissa was suddenly there in front of them, with their friends Sarah and Jules in tow.

'You took your time!' she yelled. She smiled at Annie. 'Hi-i. It's Annie, isn't it?' Annie nodded and smiled. Melissa turned back to Pia and Seph: 'The guys are over here. Come on!'

And they were off, round the edge of the dance floor. Seph followed slowly, feeling sick. Faces flashed past, a few of them familiar, most of them not. Leaning in to one another, talking, laughing. One face up against another, pashing heavily. So soon in the evening. And a teacher, frowning, pushing through . . .

And here were the guys, over the other side. Seph

tried to smile. Wez's face, so big and white in the lights. And Pak, eyes darting, hands in pockets, feet doing a kind of soft-shoe shuffle. And . . .

Where's Tom?

She looked quickly from side to side; he was definitely not there. Pak and Wez were hemmed in by the backs and sides of strangers who were facing away, talking to their own groups.

His absence felt almost physical, like a hole. Seph had to stop herself reaching forward and touching empty space.

Where *was* he? Surely someone'll ask, she thought. (Definitely not her.)

The others were talking, or trying to.

'Only 'bout ten minutes,' shouted Pak. His head jerked back over his shoulder; his teeth flared white at Pia. 'Look who's here – he's been waiting for you.'

Pia leaned forward and peered over his shoulder; Simon turned from a group further back and their eyes met. They smiled and started to move towards one another. Under the lights their movements were flickering and disjointed, like a slow motion lovers' reunion in some corny movie.

'Aw, shucks,' bellowed Wez, 'ain't love grand?' He nudged Seph. 'Eh, Seph?'

Seph made a face, distractedly. Melissa came out with some loud crack or other.

So now it was up to Annie.

'Where's Tom?' she shouted, finally.

Under the strobe Wez's shrug seemed to go on forever.

'Dunno – he said he was coming.'

And then in the next flash his face was starting to smile, over Seph's shoulder.

'Speak of the devil – here he is!'

Everyone jerked their heads around, puppet-like. Except Seph, whose stomach lurched instead.

'Hey, Tom!'

'Tom!'

Seph made herself turn her head, not too fast. Saw Sarah, Pak, the side of someone's head and then – him.

He was smiling at something Melissa was saying to him, one hand in his pocket, leaning in to catch it.

And then he looked across at Seph; their eyes connected. Only for a second, and then he'd turned, was laughing at a remark of Pak's.

Seph's heart had leapt, about as high as a bungy jumper in reverse. That look, a look of . . . what? She could hardly breathe.

'Hey, guys.' Pak was doing a twitchy hoola-hoola, arms in the air, fingers clicking. The music had changed; Jamiroquai pulsed. 'Gotta dance . . .'

Tom was going to ask her to dance, she knew it. Had to stop herself looking at him, moving towards him in anticipation. She tried to smile at whatever it was Wez was saying to her.

Suddenly she registered that Pia was standing there, with Simon. Holding hands with him, her face aglow. 'Hey,' she cried, leaning in to the group, 'you lot coming to dance?'

Seph risked a sideways look at Tom.

And couldn't believe what she was seeing.

He'd turned to Sarah and was asking her to dance.

Sarah was nodding and smiling at him. And the two of them turned away together, towards the floor.

⟿

Later, in the loo.

Seph sat bent over on the closed seat, arms clutched across her stomach, tears pouring silently down her cheeks. She sniffed and scrabbled in her bag, but she'd run out of tissues. Grabbed a handful of toilet paper, but it was no use – the tears just kept welling up and spilling over. Her throat was aching; she sobbed and gasped for breath.

And all around her were banging doors, flushing toilets, running taps and cheerful voices calling out to one another or giggling confidences to one another into the mirror. 'So I told him to get stuffed . . .' 'Anyone got a brush? . . .' 'That girl with the lacy top . . .'

How on earth was she going to walk out of there without everyone falling silent and staring at her – her with her puffy cheeks and bloodshot eyes? And once she'd made it through the door, how could she creep to the entrance and persuade a teacher she was feeling sick and needed to go home – without her friends seeing her? They'd probably still be standing just outside. At least one of them would spot her instantly and call out. And then they'd all look around and see her wrecked face . . .

'Hey, Seph, you okay? What's *wrong*?'

They'd crowd around and Tom would look at her and know.

Seph screwed her eyes shut tight and clenched her fists, her whole body stiff with misery. How on earth she could've been so stupid, to imagine that he would be remotely interested in her – of all people! That look had probably just been to confirm what he'd been *told*, if not by Pia herself, then by someone who Pia had told.

Pia, bloody Pia. How could she even think of her as a friend?

But maybe Pia hadn't said anything to anyone. Maybe she didn't *need* to. Had it been that blindingly obvious, right from that day on the beach? They'd probably all have known then, been shaking their heads and smiling: 'Poor old Seph; she's sure got the hots for you, Tom!'

Seph, sitting in her cubicle, gave a small whimper of pain.

Suddenly, to her horror, there was a voice outside, calling her.

'Seph? You in there? Se-eph.'

Annie – it was Annie. Right there, on the other side of the door.

Seph froze, her heart pounding. She stared blankly at the words graffitied on the back of the door. *Caitlin P is a slag*.

'Kate?' she heard Annie ask. 'Have you seen Seph? You know, Seph Harkness – goes to St Anne's?'

Small silence; 'Kate' must've been shaking her head.

Someone asked, 'What's she look like?'

'Oh . . . brownish hair, medium height, medium build . . .'

Ms Totally Average, in other words.

Seph sat there, very still. Nobody, she thought suddenly, would ever love her.

Another silence. And then:

'. . . think someone's been in *there* for ages.'

Seph held her breath. Then she thought to pull her feet up, out of view, but it was too late.

Annie's face was already peering, upside down, under the cubicle. Seph saw her eyes go wide at the sight of Seph's telltale slip-ons, the new ones with the purple beading that Annie had so admired when they were getting dressed.

'*Seph*?' She banged on the door. 'You okay?

'Seph, what's the *matter*?'

Later still, on a low brick wall outside. Annie was sitting with Seph while Seph waited for Nick to come and pick her up. Susan had gone out, and Seph was certainly not going to hang about till Pia's mum came to collect them. Luckily Hedy was staying with Nick and Lisa, otherwise they probably wouldn't have been at home on a Saturday night either.

A warm breeze stirred the leaves of the Moreton Bay fig overhead; music boomed from the hall. They heard a cheer go up, some whistling and stamping, then more music. They're having a great time, thought

Seph dully, and somewhere amongst them Tom was dancing with – who?

The fresh shaft of pain going through her was almost physical, like a knife.

'Feeling a bit better now?' Annie's hand came up and briefly rubbed at her back.

Which of course instantly made Seph's tears brim again. She nodded, minutely, turning her head away slightly and biting her lip. Took a huge breath, wondering if she was going to be sick after all. It would at least make her murmurings about a stomach upset more believable.

'Sure you don't want to change your mind, come back inside again?' Annie's voice was gentle; she cocked her shadowed face towards Seph's. 'I'm sure your dad would understand –'

'*No.*'

It was almost a sob. Seph shook her head hard.

Right now she'd almost rather have her fingers broken, one by one, than ever set foot inside that hall again.

CHAPTER 6

When Seph woke up the next morning it was raining. Pouring. Water drummed on the roof and dripped steadily from the gutter above the bedroom window. A myna bird huddled silently on the ledge outside, its head pulled down into its body.

She lay there, curled up, staring blankly at the empty tangle of sheets on the other bed. Hedy would've been up for ages; there was a choppy racket of cartoon gunfire coming from the living room.

Her eyes roamed the bare walls, the white ceiling. She and Hedy, she supposed vaguely, were probably just about the only people who ever slept in there.

She closed her eyes, trying not to think about last night. But it all came back anyway, like a horrible rush of nausea. As though it were the sickness she'd had to pretend about to Annie and the teacher on the door; not that it'd been very hard. By that stage her stomach was in such a knot it was amazing she *hadn't* thrown up.

She bit her lip, fighting back the tears. It was almost worse this morning. Pain and humiliation burned through her like a fire.

Desperately she tried to keep the image of Tom's face at bay, but the memory of his eyes kept returning, locking for that brief, heart-lifting second with hers . . .

Seph gave a tiny cry. That look, she realised now, had contained nothing more than pity and contempt. How on earth could she have been so dumb, got it all so pathetically wrong?

And as for the gremlin . . .

She lay there, deathly still, a fog of images swirling through her brain. For the rest of that song and the next few after that she'd danced with Wez, or with all of them in a group. She had vague memories of trying to look as though she was joining in the laughter; she must've been functioning on auto-pilot. Her real focus had been Tom – making sure she kept a safe distance, angling her body so there was no chance their eyes could meet again.

When some of them had wandered over to get a cool drink, Seph had to fight a lingering hope that he'd appear at her side, ask her to dance next time. But he'd stayed with Sarah. And then, just when she'd been wondering, heartsick, whether he really liked Sarah, he'd temporarily vanished, only to reappear – with Melissa!

That was when she'd taken herself to the loo.

Seph huddled into an even tighter ball, knees drawn up, fingers and sheet bunched at her lips. She wondered how long, if she just lay there like that, it would take her to die.

'Knock knock.'

Lisa.

Who'd already gone to bed when Seph had come in with Nick the night before. Nick'd gone into their room and borrowed one of her tees for Seph to sleep in.

Seph jerked awkwardly around onto her elbows, quickly wiping her eyes.

A hand holding a mug appeared around the door, followed by Lisa herself, that slight, quizzical smile on her face.

At home Susan always refered to Lisa as The Tart, and Seph, in a kind of daughterly solidarity, went along with it. But the nickname, she now realised with a guilty start, was really quite unfair.

'Tea?'

'Oh . . . thanks.'

Seph sat up, hands on her cheeks, pretending to yawn. 'W-what time is it?'

'About nine-thirty.' Lisa passed her the tea and stood there, her pale, almost luminous eyes looking down at Seph. 'How're you feeling?'

'Oh . . .' Seph tried to smile. 'Kind of better, I guess.'

Still Lisa stood there. Looking so . . . interesting, like someone out of a magazine, even in her cotton pants and tee.

Had she been sent in by Nick, Seph wondered, for a girl-to-girl talk? Well, bugger them both. He could come in and say hello himself. Not that she'd tell him anything.

She drew her knees up in front of her, clasping her mug on top of them.

To her slight dismay Lisa was sitting down on the edge of the other bed.

'Nick said you were looking awful.'

'Mmm.' Seph gave a tiny, wobbly laugh. 'I wasn't . . . feeling too good.'

A small, sympathetic smile ghosted across Lisa's face. They sat there in silence for a moment, Lisa's slim fingers clasped around the mug on her lap. Her nails, Seph saw, were square-cut and beautifully buffed.

'School dances can be a nightmare,' Lisa said suddenly. 'I remember one where I was so miserable I spent half the night in the loo.'

Seph stared at her.

'But I was . . . sick,' she managed finally, in a whisper. To her horror her eyes were starting to fill again. She raised a hand to her forehead and pretended to rub at an itch, then gave up and wiped at her eyes, her attempt at a laugh ending in a loud hiccupping sob.

Lisa tilted her head, the corners of her mouth turning down sympathetically.

'Oh dear. *Not* a good night.'

'Uh-uh.' Seph tried to laugh again, shaking her head rapidly. She fished around under her pillow for a tissue, located a still-soggy ball from the night before and dabbed at her eyes. She looked at Lisa again, disbelief mingling with what felt like a sudden, huge sense of relief.

Lisa – of the faint smile, the high cheekbones and the edgy suits – a sobbing teenage mess?

Another silence. Lisa stood up. 'Would you like some toast or something?'

Seph shook her head. 'No thanks.'

'Okay, see you lat –'

'Lisa?' Seph asked quickly.

Lisa turned. 'Yes?'

'Did you . . .' Seph stopped, her pride wrestling with the need to know.

Lisa stood there, looking down at her. She couldn't have been much more than thirty, thought Seph. She'd only have been about my age when I was born.

'I mean . . .' Seph swallowed. 'Why would *you* be miserable – at a social?'

She almost choked, she'd asked it so quickly. She put her mug down beside her, on the bedside table.

'Hah.' Lisa gave a short laugh. 'Boy trouble,' she said matter of factly. 'The usual shit that happens at that sort of do.'

'*You*?' Seph laughed incredulously. She'd seen the way Nick, and heaps of other males, looked at Lisa.

When her father first left, Seph used to have a recurring nightmare from which she would wake rigid and wide-eyed with terror. Nick had turned into a jolly old sea captain, smiling but almost blind, the lenses in his glasses so thick they distorted his eyes. Somewhere over the water sat a mermaid, her fishy tail wound around a rock, her eyes the colour of the curling breakers. Even though her lips were merely curved in the faintest of smiles, Seph knew that she was sending out some strange and resonant music, pitched just at Nick, sweeping him irresistibly towards her. And Seph would start screaming. But no matter how hard she screamed and yelled and tried to warn him, her father would keep right on, sailing blissfully towards that mermaid and her jagged rocks.

'Yes, *me*.' Lisa smiled and shook her head. 'I was just about the shyest, mousiest thing on two legs.'

She perched on the bed again, tucking a neat wing of hair behind her ear. 'That particular night all my friends seemed to get with guys, except me. I just stood there the whole time on my own, like a dork. I couldn't even dance in a group.' She shook her head, her eyes clouding momentarily. 'I'll never forget it.'

'Well the boys must've been *blind*,' said Seph. A thought struck her. 'Were you – did you have bad skin or something?'

Lisa shrugged and shook her head. 'No more than anyone else.' She laughed. 'I don't really think I looked *that* different to what I do now.'

She saw the disbelief in Seph's face and laughed again. 'Actually, I found the whole school thing a bit of a nightmare,' she said, lacing her fingers around her knee. 'It was only when I got out – went to uni – that I really started to enjoy myself.'

It was Seph's turn to make a face. 'Yeah . . .' She rolled her eyes. 'Uni.'

She wondered if she'd ever get there herself.

Another shrug from Lisa. 'It wasn't as though I led a particularly wild student life or anything. Although there were some pretty good parties.' She smiled. 'It was just . . . I found some people I really clicked with and the work was interesting.'

Well, you must've worked hard, thought Seph. Lisa, she knew, had recently been made a partner in her city law firm.

'So,' Seph asked, 'did you go out with lots of guys – at uni?'

Lisa smiled. 'A few . . .' She trailed off, thinking. 'But somehow it wasn't such a big issue by then. The whole thing seemed more . . . relaxed. We used to hang out in big groups in the refectory and talk for hours.'

Another shrug.

'I guess I'd become just that much older and more confident of who I was, that's all.'

'Older and wiser, eh?' said Seph. She grinned. 'It sounds like that song in *The Sound of Music*!'

Just then her father stuck his head around the door. 'What are you two nattering about?'

'None of your business!' they cried, almost in unison.

'Well, excuse me for interrupting, but I thought we might all go out and get a spot of breakfast, at Renny's or somewhere.' Nick inclined his head towards the living room and smiled at Seph.

'*If* we can get your sister unglued from the television set!'

'What are you studying in the way of Shakespeare this year?' Nick asked Seph, his eyes scanning the menu.

Rain lashed the windows; across the road surfers sat

in their cars staring disconsolately out at the choppy, foam-flecked ocean.

What on earth have Eggs + the Works, or Blueberry and Buttermilk Pancakes got to do with Shakespeare, Seph wondered.

She'd always been surprised by her father's apparent ability to think about two completely different things at once. One Sunday the year before he'd gone on writing an opening address to the jury while at the same time helping her with a long and difficult Latin translation. Of course he was forever losing his glasses, his wallet and his car keys, but he was certainly a whole lot brighter, she thought, than that creature called The Average Man that Susan and her friends loved to shriek and snort about when they got together.

'Midsummer Night's Dream,' said Seph, looking across at the blackboard specials. She was suddenly starving. The last proper thing she'd had to eat, she realised, was a cold leftover tortilla at lunchtime the day before.

Nick smiled. 'A Midsummer Night's Dream, eh?'

'Once I sat upon a promontory . . .' he suddenly declaimed, in what Seph called his barrister's voice:

'And heard a mermaid on a dolphin's back
Uttering such dulcet and harmonious breath
That the rude sea grew civil at her song . . .'

But Seph had become painfully aware of the waiter standing there at his elbow.

'*Dad*!' Her face colouring, she cast an apologetic glance at the waiter. Who, she registered with a sinking heart, had spiky hair and looked cool.

But the waiter was grinning at Nick.

'And certain stars shot madly from their spheres,' he continued, 'To hear the sea-maid's music.'

'Encore!' shouted Hedy, clapping wildly.

Lisa looked up and smiled, a finger on her lips.

'Oberon,' said the waiter, making a little bow to Hedy and whipping a pen from behind his ear. 'Some dude, eh?'

'You certainly seem to be familiar with him,' said Nick, smiling his bemused, raised-eyebrow smile.

'Played him last year in our drama school graduation play.' Joe Cool shook his head. 'What a buzz!'

'No doubt.' Nick's glasses glinted as he looked down again at the menu. 'Is the smoked salmon Tasmanian?'

Seph stared at the waiter as he took their order. What drama school was he talking about, she wondered. He didn't look much older than her. Surely it couldn't be NIDA? He seemed vaguely familiar; she wondered if she'd seen him on telly.

Hedy had fallen under his spell completely; her face had gone all pink and shiny.

'I'll have a double chocolate milkshake,' she said, beaming up at him, 'and . . . scrambled eggs plus the works.'

'Hedy,' Seph cried, 'you won't possibly be able to eat all that!'

The broad face swung around.

'Yes I *will*!'

'But you don't even like mushrooms.' Seph looked at the menu. '*Or* slow-roasted tomatoes!'

'I might've changed,' said Hedy loftily.

Nick smiled indulgently at his younger daughter. 'I'm sure between the rest of us we'll be able to polish off any surplus.' He turned to Seph and Lisa. 'Won't we, girls?'

Lisa looked dubious. Seph rolled her eyes, catching the waiter's glance. They smiled at one another.

'Hey,' he said, jerking his pen in Hedy's direction, 'got one at home myself – a little sister.' He smiled at Hedy. 'That's what's finally making me clear out.'

'Oh!' Hedy's mouth dropped open with indignation.

Lisa smiled. 'I'll bet.'

But he was looking at Seph again. Their eyes met, and the two of them laughed in a sudden warm flash of complicity.

Seph wondered whether maybe, just maybe, her life might eventually turn out to be okay after all.

⟝⟝⟞

'So, girls,' said Nick, looking up from his newly heaped plate (Hedy, of course, had abandoned her meal after four or five mouthfuls), 'what's your mother been up to?'

'Working,' said Seph and Hedy together.

'What else?' added Seph.

Nick nodded and smiled slightly, spearing some mushrooms.

'Any –' He broke off momentarily, indicating his

plate to Lisa and Seph. 'Neither of you want any of this? Delicious – shame to waste it.'

Seph and Lisa slowly shook their heads.

'Any what, Dad?' pursued Hedy, her feet kicking back and forth.

'Any . . . *men* on the scene?' Dabbing casually at his mouth with the napkin. 'Suitors?'

'You don't have to eat it all, you know, Nick,' said Lisa, suddenly cool. 'Think of your cholesterol.'

Nick nodded absently and took another mouthful.

Seph could feel him waiting. She shrugged and shook her head.

'There's Ken,' said Hedy suddenly.

Everyone looked at her.

'Ken?' said Nick. 'Who's Ken?'

'Ken?' Seph stared at Hedy blankly. Then the penny dropped.

'You mean *Ken* – from across the road?'

Hedy nodded.

Seph snorted. '*Hedy*, for god's sake!' She pictured their tall, balding neighbour giving them a cheery wave as he trundled out his wheelie bin. 'I don't *think* so!'

Her lips pressed smugly together as if to prevent any more secrets escaping, Hedy nodded again, slowly and very definitely.

There was another silence. Seph saw Lisa look at Nick.

His mouth had dropped open; for a tiny second he appeared almost stricken.

Then he caught Lisa's eye and smiled.

'Well, good for Mum, eh?' he said, winking at his daughters. 'Good for her!'

Seph had turned back to her sister, suddenly feeling hugely uneasy. 'Hedy,' she said firmly, 'Ken's *married*. You know – to Leslie.'

To Leslie the doctor, with her little white car, her nice smile and her glasses on a chain around her neck.

Hedy stared back at her.

'So?' she said finally. '*So*? That doesn't mean anything.' She shot Lisa a malicious look.

'*Dad* was married too!'

They were in the car, en route to Seph's and Hedy's place.

The rain had stopped; the humidity was building up again beneath thick quiltings of cloud. Seph's breakfast of blueberry pancakes sat heavily in her stomach. The prospect of the rest of the day was just about as unpleasant as the weather.

'Can you turn up the air conditioning, please, Dad?' she asked, opening her window. Her father glanced in the rear view mirror.

'If you put that window up again.'

Seph sighed and pulled at the button, closing her eyes and letting her head flop back against the seat. Sleep, she thought. That's about the only thing to do with the rest of a day like today.

But she had that history essay to do . . .

The seat slid sweatily against the backs of her

knees, the new leather smell of Nick's Saab making her feel faintly queasy. So different to the aroma of school bags and stale Maccas in Susan's car.

They moved forward in the traffic, then stopped again. 'So much traffic for a Sunday,' said Lisa, in between Hedy's prattling. 'Must be the end-of-summer sales.'

'Hey, Dad,' asked Hedy suddenly. 'Can we go to Timezone – *please*?'

Seph's heart sank. It was just about the last thing she felt like doing.

'Well, perhaps you might drop me home first,' said Lisa quickly, from the front.

Seph opened her eyes. 'Me too!' She turned to her sister. 'Hedy, we've been out for breakfast – that's enough!'

But Hedy was leaning forward, hands clasped in prayer. 'Please, Dad, just for a tiny bit?'

Suddenly she pointed diagonally across the other side of the intersection. 'Look! There's the entrance to the carpark – right there.'

'Well . . .' Nick gazed through the crowd of pedestrians crossing in front of the car. He made an apologetic face at Lisa.

'Could you bear it, just for five minutes? Only one or two games . . .'

There was a small sigh from the front.

'Yesss!' Hedy hissed, clenching a triumphant fist.

But Seph had suddenly seen someone approaching the crossing. Her heart lurched in horror.

'No, Dad,' she cried urgently, shrinking down in her seat. 'Please! Just drive straight on!'

Too late. The green turning arrow had appeared; the Saab was swinging slowly around behind another car towards the entrance.

Seph sunk as low as she could.

Then Hedy spied him too.

'Hey, Seph,' she shouted, 'there's *Tom* – right there!'

'*Hedy*,' muttered Seph, agonised. She put out a hand to try and stop her sister, but the combination of the chocolate milkshake, the promise of Timezone and the sight of Tom had put Hedy beyond restraint.

'Look!' She jabbed at the window, then turned and glanced, briefly puzzled, at Seph scrunched low in the corner. 'There he is.'

She pushed her window button; the glass slid majestically down.

'Hey, Tom,' she shrieked, leaning out and waving madly. '*Hi*!'

Even from down low Seph registered twenty or so heads turning. Tom's, looking startled, among them.

And the Saab had come to a halt, giving way to a car entering from the left.

'Hedy,' squeaked Seph, trying to tug at the hem of her sister's t-shirt.

But Hedy was leaning out so far she nearly fell. 'Tom – hi! It's me, Hedy!' She turned and glared at Seph, crying, 'Stop pulling at me, Seph!'

Then one more yell to Tom, extra-loud: 'Seph's here!'

So Seph had to sit up a bit, turn her head vaguely in his direction and give a feeble approximation of a smile.

Then, ridiculously, she felt herself turning to the front again and staring fixedly ahead, as though something truly fascinating was about to reveal itself in the carpark.

The Saab moved forward again, very slowly. Seph thought she might throw up, all over the new upholstery. That brief flash of Tom's face, frowning slightly, looking past Hedy to her, was printed fiercely on her brain.

As Nick stopped again and leant out to take the ticket from the machine, Hedy had one more go.

'Tom,' she yelled, leaning backwards. 'We're going to Timezone. Come with us!'

And the Saab glided forward once more, into the merciful darkness of the carpark.

CHAPTER 7

'Well, I'm heading for the bookshop,' Lisa announced as Nick pulled into a car space. She smiled at Nick, tilting her head at Seph. 'Anyone want to join me?'

Silence from the back.

'Seph?' asked Nick, turning around.

'W-what?' asked Seph, miles away.

'But, Seph,' cried Hedy, 'aren't you coming to meet Tom at Timezone?'

Seph turned and looked at her with what felt like pure hatred.

'No', she said finally. 'I'm *not*!'

Hedy's eyes widened in the gloom. 'But –'

'But nothing!' It was all Seph could do not to shake her. 'I am going,' she continued carefully, registering Lisa's offer, 'to the bookshop with Lisa, and –'

Hedy's face was a picture of dismay. 'Aaw, *Se-eph* –'

'– and I'll thank *you*, little Miss *Loudmouth*,' Seph

almost hissed, 'to keep your nose *out* of my business!'

Humiliatingly, her eyes had filled with tears – again.

There was a silence. In the front she saw Nick and Lisa look at her in the rear vision mirror and exchange glances.

'Seph,' said Hedy, staring, 'are you *crying*?'

'Of course not!' snapped Seph, her fingers dabbing at her eyes.

No-one said anything. The carpark echoed with the din of circling cars and squealing of tyres; the air was thick with fumes.

'For god's sake, Lisa,' cried Seph finally, 'let's *go*!'

Then she wondered: if he did turn up at Timezone and she wasn't there, would it look as though she was deliberately avoiding him?

On the other hand, how on earth would she be able to behave normally if he was there?

But when Seph and Lisa exited the lift into the mall, he was there; she almost walked smack into him. And instantly her heart slammed so hard into her ribcage it was as though they *had* collided.

His mouth opened, then he smiled hesitantly.

'Hey.'

'H-hey.'

It came out in a kind of croak. Desperately she tried to arrange her expression to look casually distant, couldn't care less-ish. And wasn't succeeding, she knew.

They fell silent, amid the dull roar of a thousand voices echoing to the vaulted roof. Shoppers streamed past them like water around rocks, chatting, laughing, licking at icecreams. The smell of stale donuts and recycled air was nauseating.

His brow furrowed slightly. 'Are you . . . okay?' he asked. 'I mean, when you went home early – Annie said you were sick.'

'Oh . . .' Somewhere over his shoulder a large fluorescent hotdog winked inanely.

She swallowed. Detachment, she told herself, for god's sake stay detached.

'I must've eaten something . . . I'm okay now.'

'Cool.' But something in his eyes seemed to withdraw.

She felt Lisa's gaze on them. Mind your own business, she felt like shouting at her. Don't go jumping to conclusions – even if they are bloody obvious.

Tom glanced at Lisa.

'Oh, this is Lisa,' mumbled Seph. 'Lisa, Tom.'

She'd told Tom about Lisa when they were lying on the beach that day. His tan had gone a bit paler since then . . .

Tom and Lisa were nodding to one another and saying hello.

And now he was turning back to her.

'So, you aren't going to Timezone?'

'Uh-*uh*,' said Seph, thinking instantly that this sounded too quick and emphatic. She made a twisted grimace. 'I hate those kinds of places.'

'Oh,' he said. Another pause. 'Okay . . .'

Well just go then, Seph felt like yelling. You don't have to hang around just to be nice, to make up for last night.

But somewhere deep down she couldn't quite extinguish the faint hope.

Had he in fact been heading for Timezone? Out of guilt, or —

And suddenly she had to stop herself from saying she'd go after all. It was too late now. And considering last night, *out* of the question.

Tom was looking down, pushing a flattened cigarette butt around with the toe of his sneaker.

'Well then, guess I better split.' He looked up again, at some point beyond her. 'Catch you later, Seph.'

And he was gone, just like that.

'He wanted you to go, you know,' said Lisa as they were walking through the door of Dymocks.

Seph looked at her sharply.

'Tom,' said Lisa idly, picking up a book from the specials table. 'To Timezone. It was pretty obvious, I would've thought.'

Seph shook her head, running a finger along the edge of an atlas.

'Nup,' she said in a small voice. 'I don't think so, Lisa.'

Lisa, flipping through the pages, raised her eyebrows disbelievingly.

Seph's finger was suddenly smarting; she'd given herself a paper-cut. 'Anyway,' she finally muttered, putting her finger to her mouth. 'Who gives a shit?'

She felt like pushing every special to the floor, book by glossy book.

Back home again, Seph bypassed the chilly exchange between her parents at the front door, went straight to her room and crashed on her bed. Only for a little while, she told herself. She might even read some of the play.

She lay there, quite still, staring at the dog-eared volume beside her bed. The front cover was sticking up slightly; someone had inked in every second letter of the title:

M D U M R I H S R A M.

She couldn't even find the energy to lift her hand and pick it up. She stared at her curtains, hanging motionless behind her. So hot and so close; it was as though she was drowning at the bottom of a sea of humidity.

And when Susan put her head around later to say that, by the way, both Pia and Annie had phoned this morning to see how Seph was, she found her daughter completely out to it.

Poor mite, thought Susan. The sleep'll do her good.

But Seph was running, sobbing, through a dark and mossy forest, stumbling over tree roots the size of buttresses, pitching forward and falling face down onto the damp and pungent earth. And as soon as she picked herself up and tried to rush onwards, she tripped again, barking her shins and crying out with pain.

She felt blood trickling down one leg, but she couldn't stop. Gremlins were after her, a swarm of them. Attracted by the blood, scuttling out from among the roots, flying in at her from the sides, brushing her face with their dry and papery wings. Chattering and whispering and making hideous gobbling noises; one clamped itself to the hollow just under her kneecap. Its claws dug in tight, its teeth were bared, poised to bite.

She froze, her muscles cramped in terror; she seemed completely unable to bend down and knock it off. And here was another, hovering, its wings fluttering at her shoulder with a terrible softness. Grinning at her with yellow, fish-oil eyes. Its furrowed little face was completely familiar, but she couldn't for the life of her put a name to it . . .

She jerked and twisted, but it was still there. Her jaw was locked in an endless, silent scream and then she was running across computer keys, tap-tapping over the D and the F, scrambling up the E and the R to the numbers above. Finally she hauled herself right up through the screen and into the monitor. And here, waiting for her, was a life-size cut-out of her maths teacher, Mrs Dawson, frowning, her arms folded, blocking her way. She ducked around her, only to encounter Susan, and then . . . Simon.

Simon? What was he doing here, staring into her eyes like that? He was stretching out his hand, taking her fingers in his and murmuring: 'Come with me . . .'

His lips were puffy with sunburn, and peeling slightly.

'I want you to come with me.'

Agitation swarmed over Seph like an army of ants. She knew that another girl was standing there, just behind her shoulder. She tried to shake her head but it was as though her face and tongue had turned to wood. *No*, she screamed mutely, *I'm the wrong girl! It's not me you want!*

She tried to pull her hands away, but her arms seemed to be frozen.

'Forget *her*,' he murmured, pulling Seph towards him. 'It's you I love.'

His school blazer brushed against her cheek; she caught a faint whiff of cologne. His blue eyes smiled into hers.

No! She whipped away, tearing her hands out of his. She spun around; she was on the Spider at the Easter Show. *No, no, no!* Her tears were flung wide in silver arcs, sprinklers in the sunlight. *No!* Her friends whirled past, making fun, laughing at her – she was the main entertainment. *No*, Pia. *No*, Pak. *No*, Melissa. *No* – Simon. Their faces caught in frozen, split-second hiatuses of scorn and pity.

Her stomach heaved; she was going to be sick. She couldn't see Tom, but she knew he was standing there, somewhere back there in that leering, sweating crowd.

And now the Spider was starting to shudder and shake; it was breaking up. There was a scream of metal shearing metal; sparks spit and burned like catherine wheels. A leg of the Spider sliced through a painted metal car as if through cardboard. People were tossed into the air, their arms and legs somersaulting in slow, ragdoll arcs.

The screams were becoming muffled. She was being hurled towards the centre of the machine, slowly, inexorably, into the middle of those hot and meshing gears —

'*No!*'

But a fairy had landed on her shoulder, was patting at her face. Tiny hands stroked her cheeks, the touch of fingers as moistly delicate as a summer breeze. The voice was tinkling and soft.

'You're okay, Seph. Shh, it's okay . . .'

Seph smiled and stretched luxuriantly, snuggling deeper into a bed of softest thistledown. She might never get up again.

'It's only a dream,' piped the voice. 'You were having a dream.'

And Seph at last opened her eyes and looked straight into Hedy's wide-eyed gaze.

'You were having a terrible nightmare, Seph,' said Hedy. 'Shouting out all kinds of things!'

Seph, still half in her dream, stared at her sister. She swallowed. Her mouth and throat were parched, her back damp with sweat. She closed her eyes again.

'Wh-what kinds of things?' she asked finally, knowing all too well. She opened her eyes and struggled up onto one elbow, feeling a blush beginning to creep up her throat.

'You kept shouting "No!" a lot, and you were calling out peoples' names,' said Hedy, frowning.

Seph's gaze slid to the smear of icecream at the corner of her sister's mouth, the icecream that Hedy had managed to wheedle out of Nick after the Time-zone visit.

'Like — whose names?' she asked slowly.

101

'Like – a few people. Couldn't hear them all.' She shifted her weight, leaning in towards Seph. 'But I heard the name "Simon" a couple of times.'

Seph stared back at her, hardly daring to breathe.

'You were yelling at him – you were getting so upset.' Hedy's eyes were getting wider. 'Something about being the wrong girl, something like "It's not me you want!"'

Seph shrugged and tried to laugh but her heart was pounding. She stared down at the sheet, feeling Hedy's gaze still boring into her.

Waiting for the question which inevitably followed:

'Isn't Simon *Pia's* boyfriend?'

CHAPTER 8

Sunday night; voices calling through cyberspace:

tupper_wez <seph, sefi, where r you baby>
annidreama <is she ok now??>
piachicki <i rang her this arvo>
annidreama <ditto>
piachicki <but her mum said she was sleeping>
tupper_wez <dya think we shld try again>
piachicki <& she hasnt rung back>
tupper_wez <i mean was she really crook>
piachicki <nah - think we should leave her be>
tupper_wez <or wot?>
piachicki <wot?>
piachicki <i'll see her at school tomorrow
hopefully>
tupper_wez <so here we r - just the 3 of us>
melissa965 joined the room
annidreama <what about pak?>

```
melissa965 <hi guys, mind if i join u?>
annidreama <or tom the gremlin>
tupper_wez <no come in>
melissa965 <pia said it was ok>
piachicki <ive hired her as a gremlin-buster>
melissa965 <hey - what was wrong with SEPH
last night??>
piachicki <just joking>
annidreama <she was having a bad hair nite>
annidreama <wot d'u reckon?>
```

⟶

'Now,' said Mrs Ahern next morning, first period. 'The play.' She leant forward from her perch on top of the desk, her plump legs swinging. 'We're going to be doing scenes, acting them out in groups. We'll be devoting a whole afternoon to the performances in a few weeks time.'

Seph's heart sank. In groups. Involving a need to talk, laugh, and get involved, when all she felt like doing was sitting there, quiet and still. Like river water over a stone, the teacher's words flowing heedlessly around her. Not moving, ever again.

She'd deliberately arrived late this morning, so there wouldn't be time to speak to anyone. Not Pia, whose whispered 'How *are* you?' had been cut short by Mrs Ahern's 'Sit down, please', or Melissa, who'd simply looked at her. Now they were both seated a little way back, probably staring at her. With – pity, laughter, or just blatant curiosity?

The image of Melissa on the dance floor, leaning in towards Tom and laughing, twisted in her like a knife. What if the object of their amusement had been her?

Worse, what if Tom now liked Melissa? She'd certainly be keen on him, or at least the idea of him. A boyfriend would be a powerful weapon in Melissa's armoury. She thought of Melissa's frizzy cloud of hair, cupid-plump lips and big boobs. Perhaps he did like her. Stranger things had happened . . .

Seph buried her head in her hands, feeling sick.

Mrs Ahern had hopped off the desk; her round figure bounced up and down as she jotted down the first volunteers on the blackboard. 'Amy P. and Tamsin', she wrote, 'to play Act 2 Sc.i – Helena chasing Demetrius'.

'Good. A wonderful scene.' She turned on her heel, chalk poised mid-air, eyes skimming the class.

'Now, who else?'

Seph's heart sank. She sat up, folded her arms and tried her best to look attentive but theatrically unin-spired. But her lapse of concentration had already been spotted, she knew. Mrs A's gaze was like a search-and-destroy missile when it came to daydreaming.

Sure enough:

'Seph!'

'But Mrs A?' a familiar voice piped up behind her, just in the nick of time.

Heads turned; it was Pia, god bless her. Although once Seph heard what she had to say –

'Yes, Pia?'

'Well,' Pia's tone was all innocence, 'I *mean*, just

about all the scenes have male parts, right? Like, wouldn't it be better if we got some *boys* – to play the scenes with?'

There was general laughter, and cries of 'Go, Pia!' and 'Trust you, Halliday!'

'Which boy in *particular*, Pia?' came Melissa's shout, above the rest.

Seph fiddled with her pen and pretended to laugh, but her heart was starting to thump.

Mrs A raised a quietening hand.

'Thank you, Pia, good suggestion.' She pushed her glasses further up her nose. 'I did think of that, though my motives may not've been *quite* the same as yours.' More laughter. 'If we'd have had more time,' she continued, voice raised, 'it might've been a worthwhile experience to combine with one of the boys' schools. *However,* since we only have three weeks in which to complete this unit of work –'

'*Aaw* . . .' twenty-five voices wailed in unison.

Seph gave a huge mental sigh of relief.

But Pia wasn't giving up, not that easily.

'Well, what if we organise the guys ourselves, for our individual scenes?'

Desperate now, Seph turned right around and frowned hard at her, shaking her head. Pia made a tiny face back. Translation: *butt out – just because you're not keen.*

Mrs Ahern was considering the proposition, head on one side.

'We-ell, yes, if you rehearse out of school hours and the boys concerned get permission from their school to come here for the performance, I'm pretty sure the principal would give her approval.'

General cheers and applause.

Seph's head sank into her hands. The nightmare was looming, all over again.

⌒

'It'll have to be the play-within-the-play bit,' said Pia at recess. 'You know, where the country hick characters, Quince and . . .'

'Bottom,' said Melissa.

The three of them were sitting on the edge of the Science Block verandah, sucking on frozen Poppers and kicking their legs over the side. The polished concrete, as yet untouched by the sun, was deliciously cool on their backsides.

'Yeah. Bottom,' continued Pia. She twisted round to them, her ponytail swinging. 'Quince and Bottom and their mates put on the play about the romance of Pyramus and Thisbe, for Theseus and Hippolyta's wedding celebrations. Don't think many of the other scenes have got enough parts for everyone,' she added cheerfully.

Seph swallowed. 'Well, you can count me out – that's one less,' she said, staring hard at the heat haze shimmering off the lower quad.

'Se-eph –'

'No, seriously, I don't wanna do it, that's all.' She turned around to face the others. 'Why don't *you* both do one of the four-person scenes with, say, Wez and

Pak? You two could be Hermia and Helena, and they could be Demetrius and . . . what's his name?'

'Lysander,' said Melissa.

'Lysander. One of those scenes in the woods where they're all running about falling in and out of love. It'd be really good –' Seph broke off, faltering in the face of Pia's knowing gaze. She looked down at her Popper, squeezing it hard between the heels of her thumbs. 'Lot easier to direct with just the four of you,' she mumbled.

'Se-eph,' cried Pia again. She reached across Melissa and put her hand on Seph's. 'Come on! It just wouldn't be the same without you!'

Her voice was suddenly full of sympathy and under-standing, and Seph almost burst into tears all over again. And probably would have, if Melissa hadn't been sitting there, all eyes and ears.

Due to the business with the play, there hadn't, so far, been any mention of Saturday night. But now she felt a sudden, urgent need to let the floodgates open, pour out her sorrows to Pia. Postmortem the social, moment by horrible moment.

'Anyway,' came Melissa's voice, all cheery-bright beside her, 'what about Tom? Wouldn't he want to be in it too?'

Seph's heart jumped painfully; she willed her face not to redden. She dared not turn to examine the motive in Melissa's blue eyes.

If there is an opposite of 'unassuming', she thought suddenly, Melissa is it.

'Wonder if I can get Simon to be in it,' said Pia. 'And what about Annie?'

Seph sucked hard on her straw, grateful for the move to slightly safer ground. But not for long. Jules and Sarah were coming across the lawn, dodging the sprinkler. Looking straight at her, concern etched into their faces.

'Hey, Seph!'

'You okay?'

'What *happened* on Saturday night?'

Seph took a deep breath and tried to shrug. 'I'm okay now; must've eaten something, that's all.'

Her expression felt about as bright as a spent light globe.

After lunch a group of them were making their way to maths, books in arms. And here came Mrs Ahern, walking towards them up the path. Seph saw Pia smile purposefully. And felt that sinking feeling, yet again.

'Oh, Mrs A?'

'Yes, Pia?' Mrs Ahern peered at her, her white-rimmed glasses like relics from the seventies. You could almost have mistaken her daggy look for deliberately retro . . .

'We're gunna be doing the Pyramus and Thisbe scene with some boys from Grammar, and another friend, Annie, this girl from Hilldene, if that's okay.' Pia gestured at everyone, ignoring Seph's glare. 'Us four and Sarah, for starters.'

'Fine by me, girls.' Mrs Ahern shifted her weight to one side, scratching the back of one dimpled knee with the toe of her shoe. She smiled slightly. 'But don't you think it might be wise to check with the other students first?'

'Oh, they'll be in it, no question.' Pia smiled triumphantly.

'Abso-lutely!'

---

6 pm. Seph lay stretched out on the sofa, shoes and socks off, can of Coke in hand. Her unopened bag parked in the door where she'd dumped it ten minutes ago.

She was too weary and dispirited even to get up and put on a CD. The overhead fan blew her hair about her face and cooled the sweat down her front; the rough weave of the sofa felt hot and prickly on her back. She groaned and rolled slowly off onto the floor, coming to rest on her stomach. Now her back was cooler, but the pile of the rug smelt unpleasantly gritty.

The evening stretched ahead of her like a minefield, her usual bagful of homework being just the start. If she logged into the chat room everyone'd start haranguing her to join in the play scene. Pia would no doubt be signing up Annie and the boys on the phone right now. And if she didn't . . .

Seph closed her eyes and bit her lip, wondered vaguely and dismally whether it might be possible to change schools three weeks into the school year, make a break, never have to see her friends again.

Or whether it'd be simpler just to murder Pia.

She contemplated ringing her so-called friend and

abusing her, then remembered that her phone would be engaged anyway.

She heard Susan's car pulling in at the front. Hedy's favourite Britney Spears CD boomed out; the engine died. Car doors opened and slammed shut.

Then from across the narrow street came the familiar Monday night sound of a trundling wheelie bin.

Seph propped herself up on her elbows and listened, one finger tracing the glowing patterns of the Persian rug.

'Hi, Ken!' Hedy shouted.

'Hedy,' Seph heard Susan's voice smile in protest, '*Mr Bray* to you!'

'Oh, Ken, please!' came the faint but deeper male rumble. The bin was bumped down on its haunches. '"Mr Bray" makes me feel positively elderly!'

Well, thought Seph, you must be at least fifty. She pictured their neighbour standing there smiling, with his high, sloping forehead, protruding teeth and slightly stooped back.

Hedy's carry-on about him in the cafe the day before had been ridiculous, surely.

'Don't we all feel ancient,' cried Susan. 'Don't we all!'

There was polite laughter. Weird, thought Seph, how parents moaned and groaned so endlessly about their age, when she and her friends were dying to be older. Was there ever an age that was just right?

'Isn't it hot!' Susan exclaimed. 'Any change coming, d'you know?'

'I haven't heard –' started Ken, but he was interrupted by Hedy.

'You're so lucky,' she shouted, 'having a *pool*!'

'Hedy –' started Susan.

'Heavens,' cried Ken quickly, 'come and have a swim! No, please, I *insist*. Seph too, if she's home. You know it's a standing invitation.'

Seph lifted her head. A swim would be bliss.

Susan was making the usual adult noises of demurral. 'No, really . . . very kind but we don't want to bother you.'

Seph leapt to her feet, ready to hurry out the front door and plead with her mother, but Hedy was beating her to it.

'Oh, *Mu-um*,' she bawled, 'it's just so *hot*!'

Small silence. Susan sighed.

'Well, okay then,' she said at last. Pause.

'Thanks, Ken, that'd be lovely.'

———

Water splashed from the lion's head fountain down one end of the pool; ivy climbed the umber-coloured walls. Seph floated on her back, motionless, fingers dangling like weeds through the soft green of the water.

It's like something out of *Vogue Living*, she thought; a little inner city oasis. Beyond the rustling backdrop of plane trees a faint hum of traffic hung in the pinkish evening air.

Splaaash!

Hedy bombed mightily into the water next to her, almost exploding Seph's eardrums.

'*Hedy*!'

Her sister surfaced, spat water, grinned, and set off crookedly down the pool, arms flailing, head weaving from side to side.

'Hedy,' cried Susan, 'there won't be any water left!'

'Beware Hedy Harkness,' said Ken, 'the urban pool emptier.'

For some reason Susan seemed to find this funny; Ken chortled again. His Adam's apple bobbed up and down; his big teeth flared in a grimace of hilarity.

Seph stared at the two of them and frowned, unease fluttering inside her like a moth at a screen. There did seem to have been an awful lot of . . . weird gaiety going on between them. Chuckling and treading water and bobbing up and down. They reminded her of two laughing clown heads in a sideshow.

And it was so ridiculous the way Susan never got her hair wet. While everyone else had been diving and swimming and ducking underwater, her mother merely waded in from the steps and executed a stately lap or two of breast stroke, her laquered coiffure held high above the water.

Seph lifted her hand and whacked a spray of water at her.

'Hey!' squeaked Susan, putting a hand to her hair and arching her eyebrows theatrically. 'Stop that. My perm will be *ruined*!'

'Good!' yelled Hedy, splashing wildly from the side.

Susan and Ken blinked and gasped and laughed in the onslaught, their mouths opening and shutting like stranded fish, till Ken finally lifted both hands and shovelled bucketfuls of water back. Then Seph joined in; the whole pool became a maelstrom of splashing and shrieking.

'Perm's not much good now, Mum,' Hedy cried during a lull in hostilities. She hauled herself out of the pool and tore dripping around the edge, before bombing in again, almost on top of her mother.

'*Hed* –. Oh, what the hell.' Susan pushed her hair back and grinned, catching Ken's eye. Then, to Seph's amazement, she took a deep breath, duck-dived and swam the entire length of the pool underwater.

She surfaced, gasping, and turned around from the edge, shaking her head.

'Ah, that feels better!'

Seph stared at her mother with alarm. The last time she remembered Susan ducking right under like this had been on their summer holidays up the coast, with Nick.

Her hair was plastered flat and her face washed completely clean of makeup, except for smudges of mascara under her eyes. She looked so unlike her normal self; defenceless and almost . . . naked.

'Very refreshing,' said Ken, beaming at her, pinching the water from his nose. He sank down again, side-stroking towards her. 'I must say, it's the only place to be on an evening like this.'

'Poor old Leslie!' cried Susan. 'Is she having to make house calls or something?'

'I imagine so.' He couldn't seem to take his eyes off her. 'That, or hospital visits.'

'Ugh!' she shuddered, exaggeratedly. 'Who'd be a doctor!'

'Who indeed!' he laughed, spitting water.

It was as though they'd taken happy pills, thought Seph. Or inhaled laughing gas. They couldn't seem to stop smirking at one another.

Seph thought of Leslie, tootling about visiting patients, and of Nick at Renny's, quizzing Hedy about Susan's love life. She suddenly felt sick.

'I'm getting out,' she said loudly. 'It's getting quite cold.' She swam to the side, hauled herself out and grabbed her towel off the wooden seat by the wall.

'*Cold*?' cried Hedy, from the middle of the pool. 'How can you be cold?'

Seph wrapped herself in her towel and stared at her sister, happily paddling about on a Lilo. Wondered how on earth she'd got wind of this revolting . . . *something* that appeared to be developing between their mother and Ken Bray.

'Se-eph,' sang Hedy, 'it's too hot to be cold!'

'Well I am, that's all – freezing. We've been in for ages.' Seph held the towel up to her face, breathing in the comforting smell of clean cotton.

'Mum?' she said, swinging around. 'I've got a ton of homework.'

'Yes, we really must be getting going,' said Susan. 'Getting dinner.'

But she stayed right where she was, treading water, her arms moving beneath the surface.

'No, Mum, not yet!' Hedy rolled sideways off the Lilo into the water. 'We'll only get hot all over again if we go home now!'

'Absolutely!' agreed Ken. 'No point!' He smiled at Susan, then at Seph and Hedy. 'Now, what can I get you all in the way of a drink?'

———⟩

'Ah!' sighed Hedy, still floating about. She held a glass of lemonade on her stomach; the other hand trailed in the water. 'This is the life!'

But Seph was looking across at Susan and Ken, sitting side by side on the seat, sipping their wine and smiling at Hedy. Ken's arm, casually stretched along the back behind Susan, could almost have been around her shoulder.

Hedy turned her head and looked at the two of them.

'Now,' she said, greenish reflections rippling faintly across her freckled face. 'Admit it. Wasn't this a great idea of mine – to have a swim?'

———⟩

'Hedy,' said Seph, coming into Hedy's room. 'Mum says you have to turn the light off now.'

Hedy, her hair still slightly damp, looked up from the adventures of Harry Potter. Her ancient friend Dog, his coat worn almost right through in places, was sitting as usual beside the pillow.

'Okay,' she said, yawning hugely and rubbing her eyes. She marked the page with her galah feather bookmark, closed the book and obediently snuggled down among the sheets.

'G'night,' she murmured, reaching for her lamp switch.

''Night,' said Seph, amazed at this turnaround in bedtime behaviour. It'd be so good if Hedy could get exhausted swimming every night!

But not at Ken's place. Not with Susan there, anyway . . .

'Hedy,' she said, taking a few steps into the room, 'just one thing. How did *you* know –'

She broke off, biting her lip. Hedy's face stared back at her through the shadows.

'I mean,' said Seph, coming and perching on the side of the bed, 'what made you think that there was some sort of . . .' She broke off, lowering her voice. '*Thing* . . . going on between Mum and Ken? You know, what you were telling Dad at Renny's yesterday.'

Hedy propped herself up on her elbow, her eyes gleaming strangely.

'I didn't think anything,' she said with a little smile. 'I made it up.'

Seph stared at her.

'But . . .' Her thoughts had stalled; nothing seemed to connect with anything else. '*Why*?'

Hedy fell back onto the pillow, staring up at the glow-in-the-dark galaxy of moons and stars on her ceiling.

'To make Dad jealous, of course. To make him want her back again.'

'*Hedy* –'

But Hedy was turning to Seph again, her eyes huge.

'But it looks like it's coming true,' she whispered, 'doesn't it, Seph?'

She edged closer, a tiny smirk playing about her lips. 'Mum and Ken – reckon I've put a *spell* on them!'

CHAPTER 9

Next morning, 7.15. Seph'd been standing, motion-less, in the shower for three minutes, or maybe it'd been more like ten. She wouldn't have known; her mind had wandered.

Back to the previous night. The awful carry-on between her mother and Ken Bray. Her own avoidance of the chat room . . .

And Pia's inevitable phone call, at 10 pm.

'Annie and Wez and Pak think it's a great idea about the scene – they're getting permission.'

'Yes, but –'

'And guess what? Simon'll probably be in it too if it doesn't clash with his debating dates!'

'Mmm.'

But what about –

'Tom didn't log on last night. Annie's going to tell him about it.'

Why didn't he?

'And no Gremlin either – he and it are obviously one and the same thing.'

The gremlin . . . oh please, no, don't let the gremlin be Tom.

'It's gunna be so much fun!'

Now it's all come back again. I feel sick.

'You will be in it, won't you, Seph?'

'Seph?'

'Mmm?'

'It might get The Romance going – with Tom.'

Seph breathed in sharply.

'Look, Pia, forget about Tom! I'm sorry I ever mentioned it! I *don't* like him any more. It must've been some . . . momentary . . . craziness. I just want to forget the whole thing. *Okay?*'

On the other end, silence.

I'd like to reach a long arm down the phone and strangle you, Pia.

'And P?'

'Yeah?'

'If you've said *anything* to Annie, or anyone else –'

'No-o! Course I haven't! I wouldn't say a word!'

Like hell, thought Seph now. She stood there, water pouring over her. Like bloody hell.

What she really felt like doing was melting right away, down the plughole. Floating down the storm drains, a tiny speck of nothing, into the wide blue sea . . .

Bang, bang! The door was suddenly being pounded, the locked doorknob rattled. Seph gave a start, inhaled water sharply up her nose.

'Seph! It's seven-twenty! We are leaving in *fifteen*

minutes! If you're not ready I'm going without you.'

'*Okay*, Mum, just coming.' Seph reached for the taps. Shampooing would have to wait till tomorrow.

Wrapped in a towel, she was just opening the door when she heard the phone ring.

There was a stampede of small feet; the study phone was picked up.

'Hello? Oh hi, Dad!'

Seph paused in the doorway and listened, hair dripping.

'No, we didn't get home till *really late*.' Hedy's voice was low and conspiratorial.

'We went for a *swim*.'

'Yeah, it was so hot —'

'Dunno. Getting dressed, I think. Dad? It was just *so* much fun swimming —'

'*No-o*! We just went across the road.'

'Yes.' Dramatic pause. 'To *Ken's*, of course!'

'First rehearsal's Friday night,' cried Pia, en route to class, first period. 'My place, seven-thirty.' She pointed a stern finger at Seph. 'Be there!'

Seph tried to edge past her; Pia blocked her way.

'Se-eph!'

Girls dodged around them, books clasped to uniformed chests. The second bell started ringing. Seph ducked the other way; Pia did too.

'Pi-a!' Seph was starting to giggle, in spite of herself. 'Let me through! I can't be late for Dawson again!'

'Look, Seph.' Pia's force was like a magnet, thought Seph, sucking you in. People (especially boys) got swept up like iron filings in her wake.

Seph made a last mighty effort and succeeded in breaking away, barging around Pia. She raised a hand.

'Talk about it later, P, talk about it later.'

—)

Seph managed to occupy herself for practically the whole of recess buying another French dictionary in the school shop. Her old one seemed to have vanished for good. She put the new one on the account and hoped Susan wouldn't notice. But she knew that it was just putting off the inevitable. There was no way she was going to be able to avoid Pia at lunch.

Sure enough, come 12.50:

'There you are, my darling!' The voice was sickly sweet in her ear; the arm came clamping around her neck like steel. 'You can't get away from Pia, you know!'

'Unfortunately!' giggled Seph, in spite of herself. Pia let go of her neck, linked an arm through hers and marched Seph across the north lawn, towards a shady spot under a big old fig tree.

Sometimes she wondered why Pia always sought her out, had to have her as a friend. Half the time they annoyed the hell out of one another.

But deep down, despite the irritations and the jealousies, she knew the bond was as strong as a thick band of unperishable elastic. If one of them pulled away, the other was always there to pull her back again.

It had been like that since the first day back in Year 7, during a heat wave, when Pia spotted Seph cooling off under a sprinkler. It was the kind of thing Seph did in those days.

'You'll ruin your lovely new uniform and shoes,' Pia had said, her voice deadpan. 'I can see you're a bad girl.'

She had already, Seph noticed, collected a couple of other girls in her wake.

'You're with us,' Pia had announced, jerking her thumb over her shoulder. 'Come on.'

Seph couldn't imagine losing touch with Pia, ever. But right now, infuriatingly, the elastic had no stretch left at all.

'No more nonsense,' said Pia as they plonked themselves down on the cool earth between two curving roots. 'You're coming to rehearsal, and that's that. It's all settled, everyone's going to be there –'

'Except me.'

'Oh, for god's *sake*, Seph –'

'I just don't think I could face it, that's all.' Seph yanked off her lunchbox lid and stared down at the contents. 'It's just been . . . all too much.'

How else to explain the nightmare that the weekend had been?

She picked absently at her sandwich, feeling Pia's eyes boring into her. Across the school the voices of six hundred girls rose and fell like currents in the breeze, shrieking, laughing, buzzing with gossip.

Pia sighed.

'All right then, forget about Tom! I thought he liked

you, in the holidays, but . . . well, maybe he's changed his mind!' Her arm came around Seph's shoulder and she gave her a hug. 'Who *cares*?' she cried cheerfully. 'Plenty of other fish in the sea!'

Seph twisted away angrily. I care, *I* care, she felt like shouting. And: *which* other fish? Plus, even if she did know many other half-decent boys, how could she stop her mind turning again and again to Tom? It was like some strange kind of sickness, a mental illness . . .

Then she had another thought.

'Why?' She swung around to Pia, suddenly filled with fear all over again. 'Have you heard anything – about him? You really haven't said anything, have you, to anyone?'

'No-o!' Pia, unwrapping her Lebanese roll, tossed her hair over her shoulder. 'I *told* you, I haven't.'

But she wouldn't look Seph in the eye. Instead she waved to some passers-by.

'Hey, guys.'

Seph half smiled at the others, hardly hearing a word of the ensuing chat. She was feeling about as furious and powerless as a thwarted toddler.

And suddenly she had an inkling of what it must've been like for Hedy, when their parents split up. Hearing snatches of half-understood conversation stop when you came into the room. The too-smooth words of adult reassurance starkly contradicted by the awful sounds of late-night sobbing and shouting that came seeping through the walls. And then the aftermath; that terrible vista of the damage, after the dust had settled.

Daddy's not going to live with us any more.

The terrible, awful finality of it all.

Tom's just not interested in you; he never really was.

Seph leant back into the great encircling arm of the root and closed her eyes.

'Okay,' she sighed when the other girls had moved on. 'Okay, Pia.' She suddenly felt all floppy, like a rag-doll. 'What time – on Friday night?'

So, now she was trying to be resigned to it. Accept it, Seph, she told herself – he couldn't care less. There's nothing there, nothing between the two of you. Don't even think about him. Get a life.

But that didn't stop the dreams. The more she tried to push and pull and rearrange her thoughts, like bulky furniture in a too-small house, the more the dreams intruded. Destroying her sleep, like termites munching walls. Moving in a solid layer between wake-fulness and sleep, making her cry out and wake up, all sweaty, her eyes wide. Insinuating themselves between the earliest bird call and the blaring of her alarm clock, so that she climbed out of bed dazed and uneasy, her mornings beginning already out of kilter.

Example:

Someone (was it her?) was hurtling through dense trees, rushing after someone else. She couldn't quite recognise the person being chased, even when he occa-sionally glanced back over his shoulder at his pursuer with a heart-shrivelling look of pure scorn and hatred.

And now she seemed to have shrunk into her own head; the sound of panting and feet crunching on gravel reverberated through her whole body. As though through a camera lens she watched her own fingers stretch out and touch his flying shirt and his smooth jaw . . .

And then he wasn't there.

She sat on the grass and cried and cried. Hot tears scalded her cheeks; her misery and humiliation were total. Across the way a flock of seagulls rose in a cloud and there was Lisa, with . . . Simon, lying on the grass, pashing! Their arms wrapped around one another, their lips locked in an endless kiss.

But suddenly Simon looked up and saw her. And then he was jumping up and rushing over to her and standing there, right in front of her. She tried to push him away, but he was gazing deep into her eyes, and now he was bending forward to kiss *her*.

It was Pia standing in the background, her hand to her mouth, frowning slightly. 'Don't tease her, Simon,' she called. 'She's been through enough. Don't tease her −'

Enraged and completely helpless, Seph whipped away from him, but Simon was seizing her in a gentle headlock, around the neck. 'Come with me,' he murmured. 'Come with me. You're coming with me to rehearsal.'

And some other boy was standing there too, waiting *his* turn for a kiss. It was . . . the waiter from Renny's! She recognised him by his sparky eyes.

He grinned at her. 'Hey, Seph −'

'You're all making fun of me,' she screamed. 'You're all in on it; you're making fun of me!' She was sitting on a toilet seat, a closed one, in a cubicle. The two boys were crowding in on her, laughing . . .

Cappo's was just outside, where the washbasins should have been, and everyone was sitting around at the tables, joining in the hilarity. Pak and Wez and Annie and even Leonie. They leant back in their chairs and took notes, and laughed till they cried.

At Persephone Harkness, the laughing stock of the whole world.

It was Friday night, 7.25, and Susan still hadn't arrived home. Seph had been due at Pia's at seven. And from not wanting to go at all, Seph was suddenly consumed with anxiety that she'd miss out altogether.

There was no-one answering at Susan's office, and her mobile was switched off, impervious to Seph's furious messages. Seph would've caught a taxi, but what would she have done with Hedy? There was no way she'd drag Hedy along to a gathering of her friends, *ever* again.

Seph perched on the edge of the sofa, arms folded, foot jiggling, paying hardly any attention to the rerun of *Seinfeld* on TV. She'd seen this episode at least once before. Elaine was having boyfriend problems, as usual. And of course it was all very funny; the crazy antics of Jerry, Elaine, George and Kramer continually underscored with gusts of canned laughter.

The treatment of love hassles was so unrealistic, she thought. No-one ever seemed to get really hurt. It was just the usual funky reality of the TV sitcom, with problems that could always be erased with humour.

Seph tried to imagine an episode dealing with her own romantic disasters, and gave up. The audience would just end up being bored stiff, she thought, or majorly depressed, and change channels.

Beside her Hedy sat glued to the screen, munching her way through the pizza Seph had ordered in for her. What would it be like, she wondered, when Hedy started getting interested in guys. She couldn't imagine what sort of boy, if any, would be game enough to take her sister on.

'Mmm, this is good!' Hedy proffered the box sideways. 'Don't you want any?'

'No *thank* you.' It was BarBQed Meat Lovers, Seph's least-favourite variety. 'We're supposed to be getting pizza delivered to Pia's.' She sighed. 'That's if there's any *left* by the time I get there!'

Suddenly she heard the car pulling in.

'Come on, Hed – we're outa here!' Seph grabbed her bag and jumped up to switch off the television. 'Catch Mum before she gets out of the car!'

'I haven't finished my pizza –'

'Bring it with you.' Seph snatched the box from her. 'Come *on*!'

But just as they were going through their front door, Ken was coming out of his. Seph's heart sank.

Before the previous Monday, she wouldn't have

128

thought twice about bumping into their neighbour; they often did. But now . . .

Seph stared at him. Where was Leslie, she wondered. Making house calls again?

And had he been lying in wait for Susan, just behind his front door?

'Hi, girls,' said Susan, barely looking at them. She stepped off the footpath, towards Ken. The two of them came face to face in the narrow street.

'Hi,' said Susan.

'Hi.'

They stood there, smiling idiotically at one another.

Hedy gave Seph a colossal jab with her elbow. Seph frowned and jerked away, hoping Ken hadn't noticed. But there seemed to be little danger of that; he was looking at Susan as though she was the only other person left in the world.

Seph felt a jolt of real fear.

'Thanks for the other night,' said Susan at last.

'An absolute *pleasure*,' said Ken.

'Mum!' Seph cried sharply. 'I'm late for Pia's – remember?'

But neither of them seemed to have heard. A car moving slowly down the street came to a halt, waiting for them to move.

'Mum,' called Hedy, '*car*!'

Ken and Susan drifted apart again. The car moved on, the driver shaking his head.

What on *earth* could they see in one another, Seph wondered. Feisty, rather chunky Susan (she complained about never making it to the gym these days), and Ken . . . She stared at him, aghast. Stooping, bald crown nodding and shining, big teeth bared in a grin. What *could* Susan see in him?

She tried to remember what it was he did in the way of work. An art historian, was it, or something to do with a museum?

'We must do it again,' Ken was saying in his loud, rather grating voice, '*very* soon!' He stuck out his hand, as if to gauge the air temperature. 'It's actually still quite warm,' he said. 'Don't suppose you feel like one tonight?'

Susan stared at him.

'A swim, that is,' he added quickly. 'A swim . . .'

'*Oh.*' Susan laughed, running her fingers through her hair. '*Love* to, but I have to run Seph over to her friend's place —'

'Well, come *on* then!' muttered Seph.

'Leslie . . . making house calls again?' Susan asked, a strange kind of smirk on her face.

'Ye —' started Ken, but Seph'd had enough.

'Please, Mum,' she cried. 'We need to *go*!'

Susan gave a start, collected herself.

'Ah yes. Well, better go.' She smiled again. 'See you later, Ken.'

'P'raps . . . some other time?'

⌒⌐

'It'll have to be the first half of the scene at the end,' said Pia, thumbing through her copy of the play. 'Act 5 Scene 1. Starting where the yobbos put on the play for the court — that's the funniest bit.'

There were general murmurs of 'what scene?', 'where is it?' Pages were turned; necks craned to see the nearest book.

They were all in Pia's rumpus room, draped about the chairs and sofas and sprawled on the floor. All of their usual lot, plus Simon and Jules. Sarah couldn't make it, but she'd be coming next time.

Empty and half-empty pizza boxes and Coke cans littered the coffee table; through the open doors bugs swarmed and darted around the outdoor lights at either end of the terrace.

'But,' Melissa frowned, 'we haven't got enough people for all the parts. I mean, besides the players themselves, there's all the nobles who are watching.'

Without consulting the page, she started ticking them off on her fingers. 'Theseus, Hippolyta, Lysander, Demetrius, and of course the girls – Hermia and Helena. Oh, and the courtier, Philostrate.'

'Thought of all that.' Pia smiled triumphantly. 'Hermia and Helena don't actually say anything in the scene. They leave it to the men –'

'Quite right too!' cried Wez, leaning back in his low-slung chair. He laced his fingers behind his head, his stomach protruding mightily.

'Shut up, Tupper Ware.' Annie prodded his stomach with her toe. Wez doubled over, laughing.

'*So-o*,' continued Pia, frowning at them sternly, 'we can just use last-minute stand-ins for those characters, and we can start it all with Quince saying the prologue, so we don't need Philostrate. That leaves just the right number – ten of us for ten parts.'

The door suddenly opened and Mrs Halliday popped her head around the door.

''Scuse me, everyone!'

They turned and smiled at her politely.

With her dark curls and bird-like figure, Mrs Halliday couldn't have been more different to her daughter. And not only in looks.

'Piss off, Mum,' growled Pia, under her breath.

'*Sorry* to disturb you,' beamed her mother, tiptoeing exaggeratedly towards them. She nodded at the cans and boxes. 'I just thought I'd clear this away, give you a bit of space!'

Various people started getting up or leaning forward to help, but Mrs Halliday flapped her hands at them.

'No, no!' she cried. 'Leave it! It'll only take a sec – I don't want to disturb you!'

'Then don't,' muttered Pia, but Annie started stacking boxes.

'You're not bothering us, Mrs H.'

'Not at all,' added Seph.

'We haven't finished yet, Mum!' Pia cried, indicating some uneaten slices of pizza and half-empty cans.

'Well, I'll just take away the empty stuff,' chirped her mother, darting about, seizing empty boxes and cans and clasping them to her bosom. 'Tea or coffee?'

There were several polite murmurs of decline. Seph caught Annie's eye.

'Mum!' Pia almost shouted. 'You're being a pest!'

Mrs Halliday's head tilted to one side. She beamed at her daughter as though she was a precocious and highly entertaining three year old.

'Oh, P,' she said, 'you *are* a naughty thing! Isn't she?' she asked, turning to the others. 'Isn't she a naughty thing?'

Several heads nodded emphatically; there were a few embarrassed laughs.

'I'll say!'

'You're telling me!'

Seph sighed and rolled her eyes at Annie. She never failed to be amazed by what Pia, under the guise of pretend joking, dished up to her mother. And by what Mrs Halliday took from Pia. If Seph spoke to Susan like that, she'd be grounded for a week.

Mrs Halliday was almost done, her fingers stretching around her rubbish collection.

'Let me know if you change your minds and want anything.' She beamed around at them once more. 'Sorry to interrupt!'

'Here, Mum.' Pia had hauled a couple more cans from behind her on the sofa; she leant over and poked them up under her mother's chin. 'You forgot these.'

'You right?' asked Simon, jumping up to open the door for their hostess. He closed it behind her and turned around to Pia.

'Phew,' he said, his expression a mixture of disapproval and amusement. 'What kind of brat are you!'

Pia shrugged, then smiled at him.

'Yep,' she said, 'I'm a brat. Total.'

'And spoilt rotten!' added Annie.

'Spoilt rotten!' agreed Pia cheerfully. She tapped the play with her finger.

'Now, can we get back to it?'

'So, who'll be the director?' asked Tom from his spot on one side of the coffee table, leaning against the sofa.

They all looked at him; Seph quickly glanced away again. She'd already registered that he was looking particularly . . . nice.

Everyone was quiet for a second. Obviously Pia hadn't thought about the question of direction. Or else –

'I'd be happy to direct,' chimed Melissa quickly, 'if we could combine the parts of Lysander and Demetrius into one.'

There was a small silence, followed by polite dissent.

'Nah.'

'Don't think so.'

'That wouldn't work,' said Annie firmly.

Translation: Not with you directing, at any rate.

'We don't really *need* a director, do we?' Pia tucked a long strand of hair behind her ear. Her bangles tinkled and glittered; she smiled her shiniest smile. 'Can't we just *do* the scene and all *help* one another?'

Translation: I'll end up directing it anyway, plus have a nice part.

'Anyway, *I've* got some casting suggestions,' she continued, reaching for a foolscap pad and a pen. She smiled again. 'That's if you wanna hear them.'

Simon, sprawling beside her on the sofa, was regarding her with new respect. He put a finger to his lips and smiled. 'Do we have a choice?'

Pia smiled archly at him, jabbing him with her pen.

'Now,' she started, 'Quince.'

'Ah, excuse me, excuse me, please!' cried Annie in a fake American accent, raising her hand. 'Can I be the Wall? I've always wanted to, ever since we did Midsummer Night's Dream in Year 7.'

'That's when we did it too,' said Tom.

'Most schools *do* study it in Year 7,' chimed Melissa, leaning forward. 'I don't know why we're only getting round to it this year, in Year 10.'

'Well ours must be a retard school,' said Pia, rolling her eyes. She stabbed her list with her pen. '*Now*, Annie. Sure, you can be Wall.' She made a note on the pad and looked up again. 'What about Quince?'

'Wez!' cried Seph and Simon, both at once.

They looked at one another and laughed.

Wow, thought Seph, suddenly zapped. Great smile!

And all at once that weird dream rushed at her, like a dumping wave. *He's leaning in to kiss you; you can smell his cologne . . .*

She dropped her gaze, a blush pricking horribly at her face.

'Why me?' Wez was crying in mock-indignant tones.

Seph glanced up at him, just in time to see him turn to her, his plump hand on his chest, and smile straight into her eyes.

'Why *me*, Miss Persephone?'

'Cos you're round, like a quince,' replied someone, and Tom added: 'And loud, and bossy!'

'Just the person to be the leader of the low life!' said someone else.

But Seph had quickly glanced down at the lines again, her thoughts suddenly tumbling over themselves in confusion and alarm.

Surely, surely not. It couldn't be . . .

Her thoughts slithered back to that horrible night of the social. She'd been so busy thinking about . . . other things, she realised now, that she'd barely registered how many dances she'd had with him. She pictured him smiling at her, moving to the music, taking her hands . . .

Wez would be the last person she'd think of – as a crush!

Her spirits plummeted. Life was becoming like some horrible joke jigsaw puzzle in which none of the pieces could quite be made to fit.

'Bottom,' Wez cried cheerfully. 'Why can't I be Bottom?'

'No,' chimed in Melissa suddenly, 'I think *Tom* should play Bottom.'

Everyone looked at her, and then at Tom.

'Why?' asked Jules.

'*Me*?' Tom grinned in mock alarm, reddening slightly. He ducked his head down to his copy of the play and started flipping through the pages. 'Why . . . Bottom?'

Seph looked at Melissa, who was sitting there, her cheeks quite pink, biting her lip.

'Oh, I don't know,' Melissa said. 'I thought you'd be good at it, that's all.'

Pia grinned at Tom. 'Okay, Tommy boy,' she said, 'you can be Bottom.'

Tom was still trying to find the relevant scene. 'I dunno,' he murmured dubiously. 'Refresh my memory. Who the hell's Bottom again?'

'Bottom's the star of the play,' said Annie, reaching down and helping him find the page. 'Or at least he thinks he is. Plays Pyramus, a kind of yobbo Romeo. The lover of the bee-ootiful Thisbe.'

Melissa was turning an even deeper shade of pink.

Three guesses which part you want to play, thought Seph furiously. If anyone suggests she plays Thisbe, I'll kill them.

Followed by a horrible premonition.

But what if . . .?

Suddenly she could feel Pia's eyes on her. She kept her own eyes downcast, glued to the page; her heart was starting to race. It was just like being in English class, hoping she wouldn't be asked. Desperately she ran her finger down the lines –

'Moonshine!' she shouted. 'I'll be Moonshine!'

The conversation stopped. Eight pairs of eyes looked at her curiously.

'Hello-o!' said Pak. 'I just said I'd do it – five seconds ago?'

'Oh . . . did you?' In her confusion Seph caught Tom's eye; he was starting to laugh at her. Her face burned.

'Well,' she stammered, ducking her head again, 'Can I be . . . Lion then?'

'No.' Jules shook her head firmly. 'I'm the lion.' She turned to Pia. 'Remember – you promised?'

Pia nodded. Jules smiled around at everyone and shrugged.

'I'm hopeless at acting.'

'But,' said Pak, looking at the play, 'you've still got some lines.'

'Oh,' said Jules, crestfallen. 'Do I?' She looked down at the page. 'I thought it was only roaring.'

'You may do it extempore,' quoted Wez, in ringing tones, 'for it is nothing but roaring.'

They all clapped; Wez gave a modest wave of acknowledgment. 'From an earlier scene,' he said, looking unaccustomedly bashful. Adding: 'I've actually played Quince before, at my old school, in –'

'Year 7!' several people chimed in loudly.

'Once a Quince, always a Quince,' said Annie.

Seph could feel Wez smiling at her again; she half smiled, very vaguely, in his direction.

Now there were three people to avoid eye contact with. What a mess.

'*Any*way,' chirped Pia, snuggling deeper into the cushions, 'I thought *Simon*,' (sideways smile) 'seeing he's the *oldest*, could play the Duke, Theseus –'

'And you his beautiful Hippolyta, of course,' smiled Annie.

'Well . . .' Pia shrugged nonchalantly, then smiled. 'Okay.'

'So, Melissa,' said Annie, looking at her across the coffee table. 'You're a pretty good actor. You should have a part with some lines.'

Melissa smiled and gave a little wriggle of expectancy.

I hate you, Melissa, Seph thought, I *hate* you . . .

'So how about you doing Demetrius?' continued Annie. 'He's got heaps.'

Melissa's mouth dropped into a perfect O of dismay.

'But . . . he's a boy!'

'Sure,' agreed Annie cheerfully, 'and we've got too many girls!'

'And I know Sarah doesn't want many lines,' added Pia quickly, 'so she should play Lysander. He doesn't say much in this scene.'

Seph's heart was starting to gallop.

Oh shit oh shit oh no . . .

'So,' rejoined Annie, with a smile at Seph. 'That leaves you, Sephie.

'To play – Thisbe!'

CHAPTER 10

Saturday morning, Whitechapple Road. Seph, Annie and Pia were shopping.

Well, kind of shopping. Pia said she needed a top, and Seph was vaguely thinking about buying some pants, but this was their fifth shop and so far no-one'd tried on a thing.

Idly they flicked through the rack in front of them. Girls squeezed past carrying armloads of clothes; the queues at the change cubicles were two or three deep. Music throbbed; the slow twirl of the overhead fan made no difference to the stifling air.

The smell in these kinds of shops always reminded Seph of the old theatre where she'd gone for ballet lessons as a kid. Stuffy and musky, with the mingled odours of sweaty tap shoes, well-worn costumes and stale makeup.

'These are pretty funky, Seph,' said Pia loudly, holding out some ultra low-cut hipsters in purple crushed velvet.

'Mmm,' said Seph. Maybe on you, she thought, not on me. 'Mad.' She looked at the price and gave a small squawk. 'Ninety bucks! That's about all I've got left in my keycard.'

'Try 'em on,' suggested Annie, unenthusiastically.

'Nah.' Seph shrugged. 'Can't be bothered.'

Where would she wear them? Who would she be trying to impress?

'What about you?'

Annie gave her a withering look. Dumb question, Seph. Poor Annie was so tiny she'd given up on adult sizes. Esprit for Kids was just about the only brand that fitted her.

Pia was beckoning from the chunky glass display case over at the counter.

'Hey, guys, check out these *earrings*!'

The ones she was looking at were long and dangly with silver doves and hearts threaded between ceramic beads.

The girl behind the counter smiled at Pia. 'Wanna have a look?' She inserted the brass key hanging from her wrist into the lock, picked up the earrings and passed them to Pia.

'*Perfect*,' she cried in a raspy voice, 'aren't they?'

Pia nodded, holding them out in the palm of her hand.

But Annie was turning over the tiny price tag. 'They should be, for the price! Sixty-nine dollars –'

'But they're so-o *beautiful*,' Pia crooned. She held one up against her ear and peered into the small mirror standing on the counter.

'They're actually cheap at the price,' said the girl. 'The guy who makes them for us does them all by hand.'

In Bali, probably, for about twenty cents a pop, thought Seph.

'*Pi-a*,' she murmured softly. 'As if you need any more earrings.'

Pia had at least twenty pairs, at the last count. They were her downfall, she said.

'I *know*, but . . .' Pia turned around to Seph and Annie, holding one up to either ear.

'They *so*, so suit you,' said the assistant. 'Try them both on – properly.'

Seph stared at the girl, her ragged urchin cut perfectly framing her delicate features. She can't be much older than me, she thought, and yet she makes spending seventy dollars on a pair of earrings sound as trivial as buying a can of Coke.

Pia pushed the wire hoops through her ears, piled her hair on top of her head, and turned to face her friends expectantly.

They looked lovely. Most things did, on Pia.

Annie and Seph looked at her in silence.

'Yeah,' sighed Annie, 'they do look great . . .'

'If you can afford them,' said Seph.

'Have to talk the olds into an early birthday present,' said Pia cheerfully, rummaging in her bag for her wallet. 'I'm already *way* over this month's allowance.'

Suddenly Seph couldn't wait to get out of there.

'It's so hot in here!' she cried. 'Meet you outside.'

When she'd made it out the door she found that

Annie had followed her. They leant against a lamp post, idly regarding the passing Saturday parade. The expensive sunglasses, lean bodies and funky haircuts. And every third person or so seemed to be walking a dog.

'I'm buggered,' said Annie. 'Let's have that coffee soon.'

But Seph was watching an old man who was sitting on a folding stool a bit further up, against the plywood boarding of a construction site. A cardboard sign was hung around his neck with string; beside him on an upturned milk crate sat a full tin of biros. His eyes stared straight ahead, milky and unseeing. PLEASE HELP ME TO HELP MYSELF, the sign said. PENS – $1.00.

She realised she'd seen him sitting there before, but never really noticed him. People ducked around him, unheeding, as though he was a rubbish bin or a cardboard box left out on the pavement. As she watched a dog tried to lift its leg on him, narrowly missing his trousers when its owner, chatting loudly to her friend, dragged it onwards.

'That man's blind,' she whispered, pointing, to Annie.

'Yeah,' said Annie, staring. 'Poor guy . . .'

He sat there in his yellowed shirt and baggy trousers, a slight, expectant smile on his face.

'D'you think he stays there all day?' murmured Seph. He didn't even seem to have a silver stick, let alone a guide dog. 'Like, who comes and gets him?'

Annie shrugged. 'Dunno.' She stared at him, then slowly shook her head. 'It'd be so awful!'

Seph started to reach into her bag for her purse, just as Pia came bursting out of the shop, hair flying, fancy little carry bag in hand.

'If I don't have a latte this minute, I'll *die*!' she cried.

Annie had already got her wallet out, was poking about in the coin purse. 'No change,' she said, looking at Seph. 'You got anything?'

But Seph's purse was somewhere way down the bottom of her bag. She stood there, peering and scrabbling about through the usual clutter: her mobile, hairbrush, lipsticks, an old Christmas card, her address book, numerous scrunched tissues and a book she had meant (and forgotten) to return to Annie.

Pia looked from Annie to Seph. 'Come on!' she cried, taking Seph's arm. 'I've got plenty of dough – let's go!'

Seph gave up; she and Annie shrugged and followed Pia up the footpath. Seph glanced quickly in the man's money dish as they passed, then looked away again.

There were just a couple of coins – a dollar, and a ten cent piece.

'So you noticed?' said Pia. She raised the luxuriantly frothy glass of coffee to her lips and grinned slyly at Seph. 'Poor old Wez!'

'Why "poor"?' asked Seph, indignantly.

Annie and Pia rolled their eyes. Seph giggled, blowing froth off the top of her cappuccino.

'Se-eph!' the others cried, pretending to dab at themselves with their napkins. 'D'you *mind*?'

Their laughter merged into the cheerful hubbub of the cafe. Waiters edged and twirled their way through tables, the espresso machine roared and hissed behind the vase of giant spiky flowers sitting on the counter. The din of talk and the scraping of chairs rose into the air, mingling with delicious aromas of coffee and cake.

'*Poor* because he hasn't got a hope in hell,' declared Pia, taking a forkful of their enormous shared slice of hummingbird cake, 'of Seph liking him back.' She grinned at Seph. 'I *hope* . . .'

Seph made another face. 'As if!' She speared some cake. 'Just think of it – I'd be smothered!'

They all cracked up.

'Suffocated in fat,' squeaked Annie. 'Squashed – flat as a pancake,' Seph snorted, choking on her mouthful. She coughed and spluttered; the others patted her on the back and Pia handed her a glass of water.

'Poor old Wez,' said Annie finally. They all nodded, suddenly feeling quite ashamed of themselves.

'I mean, I really love him – as a friend,' said Seph solemnly, and they promptly burst into more hysterics.

But a tiny voice was crying: After what you've been through lately, you're laughing at *Wez*?

Some layers of pain, like subterranean rivers, were best left unexplored. She didn't even want to think about Wez, about that funny little kind of . . . defenceless smile he gave her.

Also, she kept thinking about that blind man.

She pushed both images away, asked: 'So how did you guys know about Wez?'

145

'Pak said something to him at the social,' said Annie, 'after you left. Something like, "You've missed your chance now, old son!"'

Seph groaned.

Pia nodded, laughing. 'We didn't say anything earlier because we didn't want to depress you.'

'Well it *is* depressing,' said Seph. True – suddenly the thought of this . . . crush of Wez's was like one more lead weight hanging around her neck. It made her feel guilty, even though she'd done nothing to encourage it.

Then she wondered something.

'What?' she asked, leaning forward and digging into the icing. 'Did he say it in front of *every*one?'

She was trying to sound casual, but Pia was onto her immediately.

'Yep,' she answered, smiling straight at Seph. 'In front of all the *boys*, at any rate.'

Seph threw her a tiny, concentrated frown of warning, her eyes slipping sideways to Annie's face. To her horror she spied a minute smile lurking there, at the corners of the Annie's mouth.

She glared at Annie, then swung back to Pia.

'*Pia*!' she cried. 'You said you wouldn't tell *anyone*!'

Pia stared back at her, momentarily caught out.

Seph gave a low, bitter laugh.

'Thanks a lot, *friend*.' Prickling with anger and humiliation she looked down, twisting her napkin tight around her fingers.

There was a tiny silence, before the other two sprang to console her.

'But, Seph,' cried Annie, her hand on Seph's arm. 'I guessed anyway! I mean,' she added hastily, 'I had a feeling he liked *you*, so . . . I asked Pia –'

'And what am I supposed to do – lie to her?' said Pia. 'How am I supposed to fool *her*, eh?' She jabbed her thumb in Annie's direction, putting a hand on Seph's.

Why did you think that he liked me? Seph wanted to ask Annie, but didn't. Instead she glared at Pia.

'How many others know? How many other people have you blabbed to?' She turned to Annie. 'To Tom *himself* by any chance?'

And to think they'd been having a good old laugh about Wez!

'*No.*' There was genuine denial in Annie's eyes. 'Of course not! I've hardly seen him since school went back!'

'Anyway,' muttered Seph fiercely. 'I don't even *like* him any more. It must've just been a thing at the beach that day.' She stared hard at them both, willing them to believe her.

If it weren't for their tiny, infuriating smiles of incredulity, she might almost have convinced herself.

Then someone bumped the back of her chair.

'Sorry,' said a girl, walking past with a couple of friends.

'S'okay,' murmured Seph over her shoulder, barely registering. But as she turned her head back to Pia and Annie, she caught the glance of one of the boys in the group. He smiled at her as though he knew her; she vaguely smiled back. Only a half-baked, preoccupied smile; her thoughts were elsewhere.

But a second later her mind sat up and took notice.

She knew that face, those laughing eyes and funky hair . . .

It was that waiter – the one from Renny's! Obviously not working today, visiting a different cafe. Her gaze picked him out again as he threaded his way through the tables towards the door, laughing about something with his friends. She wished she'd given him a nicer smile.

But he must've felt her eyes on him – he was turning around at the doorway, his eyes meeting hers. They grinned at one another; he gave her a little wave. Just for a moment it seemed as though he was going to duck back and say hello properly –

But then his friends were out the door and he was following them.

'Who was that?' asked Pia, craning her neck in the direction of Seph's gaze.

'Oh, just some guy I met somewhere,' said Seph with a little shrug. She leant forward on her elbows, her cheeks in her hands, trying to cover the sudden rush of warmth in her face.

Five minutes later.

'Hey, look,' said Annie, pointing across to the entrance.

Seph and Pia turned around in time to see Nick and Lisa coming through the door.

'Oh gawd,' said Seph, half jokingly, 'look the other way!'

'No-o!' cried Annie. 'Your dad's cool!' She stood up, waving across the tables. 'Hi-i, Mr Harkness!'

Lisa saw them and nudged Nick. They smiled and waved, started to make their way over.

'Got The Tart in tow,' murmured Pia.

'Nah,' said Seph quickly, 'she's okay.'

Several people glanced at Lisa as she passed. It's not as though she's outrageously gorgeous or anything, thought Seph. It's just . . .

'Well met, proud Persephone,' misquoted Nick, bending to kiss Seph on the cheek. 'Still doing A Midsummer Night's Dream?' He smiled at Annie and Pia, gesturing to Lisa. 'Hello, girls. You've met Lisa, haven't you?'

'Think so,' said Annie, smiling.

'Yeah, once, at Seph's place,' added Pia.

Seph would never forget it – the first and only occasion Lisa had ever set foot in the house. It had been a Friday evening and Pia and Annie had come over to stay the night. Lisa stopped by on the way home from work to pick up Hedy. Susan was still at the office.

Lisa came upstairs to help Hedy and Seph gather up Hedy's overnight things. Seph'd felt totally mortified by the end-of-week chaos; they'd spent at least ten minutes trying to find one of Hedy's missing sneakers, eventually locating it under Susan's unmade bed.

Worst of all, Susan had arrived home just as they were leaving. The memory of the taut anger in her mother's face and the icy, barely civil exchange between the two women was still enough to make Seph feel sick, two years later.

After that it had always been Nick who arrived to pick up Hedy.

Now he was looking down at their empty cups.

'Have you only had coffee?'

'And hummingbird cake,' smiled Pia.

'That's not enough for this time of day,' said Nick. 'Let me buy you all some lunch.'

'Oh no, Dad,' cried Seph hastily. 'We're fine –'

'Sit down,' Annie said to Nick and Lisa, much to Seph's annoyance. She leant over and pulled out a couple of chairs from the next table.

'No,' protested Lisa mildly, 'we're interrupting your chat!'

'Not at all.' Annie grinned at Seph and Pia. 'We've been yakking nonstop all morning.'

Five minutes later, when Nick and Lisa had ordered ham and pesto baguettes, and Pia and Annie second coffees, Nick turned to Seph.

'So, how're things?'

Seph shrugged. 'Okay.'

'School going well?'

'Yeah, s'pose.'

'And . . . your mother?' Nick leant forward, twisting his water glass between his finger and thumb. 'How's she?'

Seph thought of Susan's distracted silences during the drive to Pia's the night before; of her totally vague responses to Hedy's chatter. And how, when they'd stopped outside Pia's gate and Hedy'd suddenly asked if the two of them could please go for a swim at Ken's when they got back, Susan had started, almost as though someone had tickled her.

'Oh no, darling,' she cried, 'it's *much* too late for that . . .'

She'd trailed off, staring through the windscreen, and Seph had got the distinct impression that actually there was nothing her mother would've liked more.

Seph looked sideways at her father, still apparently fascinated by his glass. Crazy, she was tempted to reply. She's gone crazy for our neighbour, Dad.

She was suddenly reminded of Manuel, the dopey Spanish waiter in that old British sitcom, *Fawlty Towers*. 'He go crazy, Mrs Fawlty, he go crazy for that girl . . .'

Seph would always remember a hot Christmas afternoon five or six years ago when, stuffed with turkey and plum pudding, the whole family, including Nick, had sat around and watched a *Fawlty Towers* video. They'd ended up crying with laughter; it had been one of the happiest Christmases ever.

Now she shrugged again.

'Mum's okay.'

'She hasn't *really* taken up with that neighbour, has she?' Nick asked suddenly. He glanced quickly at Lisa, who was still involved in conversation with Annie and Pia, before turning back to Seph. 'What's his name?' He ducked his head, lowering his voice slightly. 'Keith, is it? Ken . . .'

'Ken,' said Seph. A fantastical thought was suddenly taking root in her brain, sprouting and shooting, despite her half-hearted attempts to crush it.

She toyed with her empty cup, feeling Nick's eyes

on her, waiting for her reply. And all at once she felt a shameful and quite wonderful sense of power.

'Well, there does seem to be *something* going on.' She turned to him and frowned. 'They do seem to have the hots for one another.' She sighed bleakly. 'Dunno what Leslie – his wife's gunna say about it.'

'Oh, my god!' Nick's mouth dropped open, his casual, couldn't-care-less pose forgotten. 'It's come to *that*, has it?'

Seph stared at him, her heart beginning to sing. The sprouting shoot had suddenly become a full-blown plant, Disneyesque in its weird and wonderful proportions. Exotically and luxuriantly leafy, uncontrollable and unstoppable.

He's jealous, he still loves her, he wants her back!

They might get back together again, forever.

Seph pictured them the next Christmas, all together again on the sofa, laughing. What was that Disney movie, where the sisters engineered their parents' reunion? *The Parent Trap*.

No, Seph, get real.

'What are you two getting so excited about?'

Lisa had abandoned her chat with the others and was looking at them across the table. 'Hey,' she asked, half laughing, 'what's the problem?'

But Seph could see anxiety flickering in her eyes. She wondered how much Lisa had actually heard.

She could feel herself colouring, but Nick quickly reached across and patted Lisa on the hand, almost absentmindedly.

'Never you mind, my sausage, never you mind . . .'

The food arrived. Seph watched Lisa as the waiter set out the plates. The normally gracious smile of thanks was barely apparent; the grey eyes, usually so steady, surreptitiously searched Nick's face for clues.

She's upset, thought Seph. And jealous.

And then it hit her.

She really loves him. This most attractive and clever young woman was actually in *love* with her rather portly, middle-aged father. Who himself still seemed partly hung up on her chubby, middle-aged mother – even though the two of them could barely be civil to one another.

And therefore is winged Cupid painted blind . . .

It's all too hard, thought Seph. I just might become a nun.

CHAPTER 11

A few nights later the gremlin struck again.

Seph, new dictionary at hand, had been struggling with a French translation from one of those hell-boring little French so-called 'teenage' magazines, really written by middle-aged teachers for foreign students. Something about discipline in French high schools, committees of mediating students. Really gripping stuff.

She'd done about half of it; thought she'd have a break. Go and make herself a little snack.

Once again she glanced at the monitor on the other end of the desk, blank and silent. By now the messages would be zapping back and forth, she knew; any minute she'd get a 'where are you?' phone call from Pia. She couldn't put off logging on again forever, she knew; didn't want to look as though she'd completely gone into hiding.

'Hedy,' she heard Susan call from the foot of the

stairs, 'is that the light still on? Turn it off now, please – immediately!'

Hedy was in Susan's bed again. How old would she be, Seph wondered, before she was finally happy to stay put in her own?

'Yes, Mum,' called Hedy. The extra glow spilling out into the hall was extinguished.

'Thank you,' called Susan. 'Now, go to sleep!' And she toddled back, Seph knew, to the sofa and her weekly date with *The Bill*.

Seph sighed and switched on the computer. Just for a few minutes, just to check.

The 'Friends in Chat' box showed piachicki (of course), and p_a_k and tupper_wez (oh-oh).

When she got into the room she saw that ToMtOm had just left, about five lines back. She felt stabs of disappointment and relief, almost simultaneously.

tupper_wez <here she is - our lil thisbe>
p_a_k <and pyramus just left>

Seph's heart jumped in fright. Cool it, she told her paranoid self. He's just talking about the play, that's all . . .

sefi_15 <shove it moonface, or moonshine>
piachicki <speaking of the play>
sefi_15 <who-everrr>
tupper_wez <doesnt moonshine have a dog??>
piachicki <did every1 agree fri nite 4 next rehearsal?>

tupper_wez <wot we gunna do for da dog??>
piachicki <we'll probly have to have an extra
1 the last week>
sefi_15 <how bout bean??>
piachicki <brill!!>
tupper_wez <poifect, harkness!>

Then:

grEMLin joined the room

Seph's heart instantly started to pound; she wondered whether to get out there and then. But surely it wasn't –

piachicki <PISS OFF GREMLIN>

But if she were to leave again so fast, Seph thought, wouldn't it just be drawing attention to herself? Wouldn't they all wonder why?

p_a_k <nice 1 tom>
p_a_k <2 log off & then come back as the
gremlin - really sub-tle>
tupper_wez <tell us something interesting 4 a
change>
tupper_wez <like WHO ARE U>
grEMLin <tom?? im not tom>
tupper_wez <or its ignore for u, buddy boy>
grEMLin <something interesting, lets see>

Seph held her breath, could hear her heart thumping.

grEMLin <piachicki, your luv lifes about to take a dive>

Seph slumped back in her chair, the pressure (temporarily at least) off her.
For once there was a small cyber-silence. Then:

piachicki <??????????? yeah?>
tupper_wez <NO!>
grEMLin <yeah your boyfrends falling in luv with some 1 else>

Seph frowned, unease pricking at her scalp.

p_a_k <not the famous simon - unfaithful already>
piachicki <like WHO, gremlin?>
tupper_wez <yawn>
tupper_wez <ignore, ignore>
greEMLin <thats for u to find out!!!!>

Then:

grEMLin left the room
tupper_wez <before we could even put him on ignore!>

'Who the bloody hell *is* this gremlin, that's what I'd like to know!' Pia dumped her bag into her locker with a crash. 'What a nerve! What on earth would he know about Simon anyway?'

'He – or she – probably knows *nothing* about you, or Simon,' said Seph, barely glancing up from the depths of her bag. Her PD textbook seemed to have gone on temporary walkabout. 'He didn't actually mention Simon's name. He's probably just making the whole thing up!'

Pia was still standing there, frowning. The second bell rang, as loud and jangling as a fire alarm.

'Probably,' she said finally, with a shake of her head and a little laugh. She looked down at Seph. 'But the whole thing still gives me the creeps, Seph – it just gives me the *creeps*!'

'What gives you the creeps?'

Melissa's face had popped around her locker door, her hair subdued into a neat French plait. Her eyes are always clear, thought Seph, and her cheeks so rosy. And she never seems to get any pimples.

Melissa looked from Pia to Seph and back again. 'What gives you the creeps, P?'

'Oh . . .' Pia's eyes met Seph's. Old busybody Melissa was at it again.

'It's nothing, Melissa. Just . . . a gremlin that just keeps turning up in Chat.' Pia suddenly swung around and looked at her. 'It's not *you* by any chance, is it?' she asked, only half jokingly.

Melissa stared back at Pia, her books clutched to her chest.

'*Me*?'

'Nah . . .' Pia gave a little laugh and shook her head, turning back to Seph. She sighed 'I guess it has to be Tom. But *why* –'

'*Ladies*!' The voice of Mrs Urquart, the deputy principal, cut into their backs. They jumped. 'If you're not in class in *one minute*, there'll be detentions for both of you!'

Pia grabbed her books and the two of them scuttled off. Melissa, Seph noticed, had already gone.

Seph was really proud of herself that night – no chat room, and no phone calls. Well, just a quick call to Sarah, to ask her about the research topic for Art, but that only took five minutes.

But the next night she had to log on, if only to keep the promise Pia had extracted from her as they were leaving school earlier that day.

Bags slung over their shoulders, their feet beating time in the surge of departing girls, Pia had started her wheedling.

'Please, Seph, just for a little while?'

Seph sighed. 'What's the point? We'll only get the bloody gremlin again.'

Pia whirled around and kept walking backwards, almost in front of Seph.

'That *is* the point! I wanna find out if he really knows anything. About . . . Simon.'

Seph gave her friend a withering look.

'*Please*, Seph!' Pia stopped so suddenly Seph almost bumped into her. 'I need some . . . moral support.'

Seph stared at Pia, amazed at the vulnerability and uncertainty clouding those blue eyes.

'*Pi-a*!' she cried finally. 'How could he, or she, know anything? Even if the gremlin *is* Tom, he doesn't have anything much to do with Simon, does he?'

Pia turned and headed forward again, jaw set grimly. 'He might know more than we think,' she said, hefting her backpack higher. She turned to Seph once more. 'He might've *seen* him with somebody else for all I know!'

Seph's gaze slid away from Pia's.

'Don't be silly,' she mumbled, suddenly struck by a wave of what felt ridiculously like guilt. She pushed it away, but later, sitting alone on the bus, the strange uneasiness came trickling back.

She'd been having these crazy dreams about Simon, and now she was beginning to feel like the 'other woman'!

She'd had another, last night.

'Please, *please*,' Simon had pleaded, pulling her close. 'I *love* you.'

It was in the park; over his shoulder she could see the seagulls again, flapping and squawking around a council employee who, looking very much like Ken Bray, was emptying a rubbish can into a wheelie bin.

'No you don't. You love . . .' Seph trailed off. She knew that she knew who it was he loved, but she couldn't for the life of her say the name. She wriggled and squirmed in his arms, but he only held her tighter.

And over his shoulder she could see that other girl prowling around in the bushes, her eyes bright with fury, circling and snarling like an angry vixen.

'Hey, I'm trying to say your name,' Seph yelled to her. Adding furiously: 'I don't *want* him, truly . . .'

But Simon's chest was wonderfully warm and his shirt smelt as though it had just been ironed.

'You want *me*!' cried Tom, suddenly there, pulling at her elbow. He turned and gave Simon an almighty shove. 'Get lost, mate! You love someone else!'

But Simon kept his eyes on Seph.

'No,' he murmured. 'I hate her! I must've been crazy to think I ever loved her!'

Suddenly there was a horrible animal cry.

'Pia!' screamed Seph. With the recognition came a moment of pure terror, the putting of a name to that looming, distorted version of Pia's face, pressing in on her like a reflection in a sideshow mirror. She saw her own scream whirl away up into the sky like a white tornado. Everything was suddenly silent, as though the volume had been turned right down.

Suddenly Pia was soundlessly hurling herself at Seph, teeth and long fingernails bared, about to bite her and scratch her eyes out. And no matter how much Seph screamed and jerked her head and tried to pull away, she couldn't escape those talons –

And then she was wide awake, staring terrified into the darkness.

So now Seph glanced at her watch: 9.05 pm. She sighed. She knew she'd promised Pia, but even maths homework was preferable to more of the gremlin.

Insane, she thought, doodling down the margin, how a cyber-ghost could wreak such havoc. She couldn't remember Pia being so upset since . . . forever.

On with the modem, in with the password, and up came 'Friends in Chat'.

But Pia wasn't even there; it was only Wez and Pak. Hanging out in the chat room, when they were practically next door to one another in the dorm.

She hesitated, then went in. Just for a little while, so she could tell Pia she'd logged on. And Pak was there, so it should, she thought, be safe with Wez.

But about six lines later Pak announced he was departing. Tactfully, Seph realised, with a sinking heart; very tactfully.

```
sefi_15 <dont go pak>
sefi_15 <stay and chat - pias logging in soon>
tupper_wez <no, buzz off>
p_a_k <no, gtg>
tupper_wez <go apply yourself to your studies>
p_a_k <yes, big mon>
p_a_k left the room
```

Pia, Pia, Seph thought desperately, where are you?

Funny, up until last Friday night she wouldn't have thought twice about yakking on for hours with Wez. But now the pause was very awkward.

```
tupper_wez <so, sephi, how's ever lil thang?>
sefi_15 <ok, i guess>
```

```
tupper_wez <just ok??>
sefi_15 <dunno where pia is>
sefi_15 <she wanted me to help her tackle the
gremlin>
tupper_wez <stuff the gremlin - we'll put him
on ignore>
sefi_15 <dya reckon its tom?>
tupper_wez <he swears 2 god it isnt>
tupper_wez <hey sefi?>
```

Seph swallowed. Here it comes, she thought, here it comes.

```
tupper_wez <wanna go to a movie or somefink
sat night??>
```

She stared at the screen, her heart beginning to race. It was only good ol' Wez, for heaven's sake – why was she getting so upset?

Because she could picture him hunched over the keyboard, that's why. A strangely nervous, hopeful look on his normally wisecracking dial . . .

Reply, she told herself, reply.

```
sefi_15 <nah, got too much homework due monday>
sefi_15 <speshly since theres rehearsals fri
night>
```

Bullshit. Imagine if it'd been Tom asking.

```
tupper_wez <bummer - praps some other time?>
```

Tell him, tell him now, for crying out loud. Just say it. Something like: 'as a friend – OK?'

But instead she just typed <maybe>.

Then quickly added: <how about that – no pia and no gremlin> <heapsa work – gtg>.

And she left.

Gutless, Harkness, you're completely and utterly gutless.

———

On Thursday night there was a terrible row.

Seph, Susan and Hedy were eating dinner – late. Susan had cooked tonight; one of their favourites, Thai chicken salad.

'Mmm, good, Mum,' said Seph, wolfing it down.

'Don't gobble quite so *fast*, Seph,' said Susan. 'And elbows off the table – both of you. I don't know what other people must think when you go to their places.'

But it was said quite cheerfully; Susan had been in a suspiciously good mood the past few days.

'But I don't *eat* like this at other people's houses,' said Seph.

It was her standard reply; they must've had this exchange about fifty times. And anyway, mother dear, she thought, if you'd have got home earlier, we wouldn't be quite so starving.

'Well, don't eat like this at home either,' chimed Susan, right on cue. 'I'm the one who has to watch you.'

She trailed off and took a sip of wine. 'Just look at

that sunset!' she said, pointing through the French doors out onto the balcony. 'Isn't it magnificent?'

They gazed out over the house behind's slate roof. Delicate strokes of deepest pink were bleeding into the darkening sky.

'Looks like melting choc-cherry icecream,' said Hedy. She twirled her noodles carefully around her fork before adding, 'This hasn't got as much chilli as usual.'

Spicy food could never be too hot for Hedy. Nick called her the chilli queen.

'Just eat your dinner,' replied Susan automatically. 'Not another word till you've finished!'

She and Seph leant back in their chairs contentedly; Susan took another sip. A warm breeze nudged at their bare skin; from next door's balcony came the delicate tinkle of windchimes.

'It's cooler tonight,' said Seph. 'Not so humid.'

'Mmm . . .' Susan's stretch was almost a purr. 'A gorgeous evening.'

Then the phone rang.

Hedy turned and reached behind her for the receiver.

'Hello?' Her face lit up. 'Oh hi, Dad!'

Seph sighed, picked up Susan's and her plates and headed for the dishwasher.

Hedy frowned, looked at her mother. 'Yeah, she's here. Hey, Dad?'

But something was up; a jolly chat with Hedy was obviously not on Nick's agenda. Seph bent down and pulled open the door of the dishwasher, feeling a sudden, queasy sense of foreboding.

Hedy handed the phone to Susan, looking miffed.

Susan put the receiver to her ear.

'Yep?'

A pause; she sighed.

'I've been in meetings all day; I didn't return *any* calls. I was going to ring you this evening –'

Long silence. Seph straightened up and stared as Susan's look of irritation changed to one of amazement, then anger, and finally rage. And she was looking at Hedy and Seph as though she was about to murder them.

For the first time that Seph could remember, Hedy announced voluntarily that she was off to bed.

Other than leaving home, homework was looking like the best option for Seph. She glanced quickly around for her bag; Hedy scuttled up the stairs.

Susan took a huge breath.

'Have you quite finished?' she asked, her voice glacial.

Then she let fly.

'What – a – bloody – *nerve!*'

Each word was like a knife hurled down the phone. 'From *you*, of all people. What an *unbelievable* cheek! Even if –'

Slight hiatus as Nick tried to interrupt, but Susan ploughed on over the top of him.

'Even *if* what the girls told you were true – though how for one minute you could take the fantasies of two father-deprived children *seriously*, I can't imagine – even if it *were* true, it's absolutely *none* of your business!'

By now Seph was flitting about the room as frantically as a trapped bat. She was just about to abandon the search for her bag when she flung open the front door and found it sitting there on the doorstep, where she'd left it. She grabbed it, slammed the door and scurried towards the stairs, her heart thumping. She glanced at her mother as she went.

Susan had gone quite pale; she was gripping the phone with both hands.

'*You*, of all people,' she was shouting, '*pontificating* on what's best for the girls!' Her jaw dropped open with incredulity. 'After what you did to us!'

Seph flew up the stairs two at a time, her mother's voice following her.

'You don't have a leg to stand on!'

Seph escaped into her room; shut the door.

But not for long.

'Persephone and Hedy!' came the cry a couple of minutes later. 'Get down here, please – *immediately*!'

Next morning things were rather subdued.

Hedy got herself a bowl of cereal and sat quietly down one end of the table. But when she looked up and caught Seph's eye, there was a strange kind of smirk on her face, the look of a puppy who'd been caught demolishing a new cushion.

Susan took a sip of her coffee, put it down again and turned and reached for the Panadols. Foil crackled loudly as she popped a couple through. She gulped them down and took a deep breath.

Here it comes, thought Seph; more mega-embarrassment.

'Now, *girls*.'

Susan stopped and stared down at the bench, as though the patterns in the granite were of major interest. She lifted her head again. 'One final word. I'm sorry that there seems to have been some sort of . . . *misunderstanding* about the . . . nature of the relationship between myself and Ken Bray, but I can assure you that there is absolutely *nothing* going on between us.'

Her gaze moved from Hedy to Seph and back again; Seph felt herself starting to blush. 'Ken and I are simply friends and neighbours, and that's *all* there is to it.'

She might've been a movie star, Seph thought suddenly, facing a barrage of reporters. *There is absolutely no truth to the rumour* . . .

'We were all just having a bit of fun in the pool that night,' Susan continued steadily. But she couldn't quite seem to look them in the eye. 'That's *all*. It was a hot night and we were all having fun. There was absolutely no question of any . . . *romance*.'

Like hell, thought Seph. What other name would you have given to such heavy-duty flirting?

But she and Hedy sat there silently, eyes downcast, biting their lips.

'So, I absolutely do *not* want to hear any more nonsense said about Ken Bray,' Susan finished, her tone suspiciously bright. 'He's married to Leslie, they're both very kind neighbours of ours, and that's that.'

Final, hard stare.

'Understood?'

Hedy and Seph slowly nodded, their eyes fixed on the grain of the table.

So what would it be like, Seph wondered, the next time she bumped into him?

CHAPTER 12

Friday night – rehearsal.

This time they'd had Lebanese takeaway. Pia's mum had again insisted on clearing away the plates and empty containers, but there was still a tang of tabouli, yoghurt and spicy meat hanging in the air.

Furniture was being shifted to create a performance space. Mrs Halliday had politely requested that everything be lifted rather than dragged, so as not to mark the parquet floor.

One of the sofas was turning out to be particularly heavy.

'Over there,' Pia pointed. 'Right back against the wall.'

Wez and Tom puffed and staggered at either end of the couch; Wez was red in the face and already starting to break out in a sweat.

It was another warm night, despite being the middle of March. Thunder growled distantly; lightning flickered over the darkly silhouetted treetops across the other side of the gully that formed a park below the Hallidays' house.

'Put it down for a sec,' grunted Wez.

'Oh, for goodness *sake*,' cried Pia, waving an airy hand, 'just push it! My stupid mother – it won't make marks.'

They straightened up; Wez mopped his brow. 'Where d'your olds get their furniture from, Pia?' he puffed. 'Bedrock?'

Simon moved in next to Wez. 'Shove over, Fred,' he said, in a passable imitation of Barney Rubble, 'you're as weak as piss!' He elbowed him out of the way and bent down to get a grip, looking up at Tom. 'Ready? One two three – heave!'

They lifted and staggered, eyes bulging, veins standing out like cords on their necks. They deposited the sofa with a thump and leant back against the wall, breathing heavily.

'My hero!' cried Pia, in mock-bimbo tones. She tripped over and draped an arm around Simon's neck, squeezing his upper arm. 'Jus' *feel* dem muscles!'

Pia was being extra flirty with Simon tonight, but a couple of times Seph'd seen her glancing his way with a little frown.

Simon smiled. 'Expecting payment, baby,' he growled in gangsterish tones. 'Later.'

Pia giggled and pretended to slap him about the face, but Seph was stealing a look at Tom. He was still leaning against the wall, his thumbs hooked in his shorts.

His eyes suddenly moved in her direction; she jerked her gaze away.

Melissa was taking charge down the other end of the room.

'Come on,' she said to Pak, patting the tops of two matching armchairs, 'let's move these.'

But the chairs weren't much easier than the sofa; it took the combined efforts of Melissa, Pak, Sarah and Seph to shift them, one after the other.

'Gee, Pia,' said Pak, flopping backwards into one of them, 'can we come back and do this again tomorrow night?'

'Next she'll be saying we should rehearse on the terrace instead,' said Wez, smiling at Seph from the other end of the stone coffee table they were both lugging.

'Hey!' Pia whirled around, staring through the open doors. 'That's not a bad idea!'

There were several groans.

'No-o, seriously!' She walked outside and turned around to face them all, the outdoor lights making a soft halo around her head. 'It's lovely out here, and we'd certainly get the feeling of outdoors!'

'But the scene's set in the Duke's palace,' said Melissa.

'Who cares?' Pia smiled. 'It would give us a real feeling of . . . the dream.' She stretched out her arms. 'And midsummer!'

Melissa frowned and folded her arms.

'It's autumn,' she said, 'officially.'

A few minutes later and the players were all out on

the terrace, cast in gentle silhouette, lips, cheeks and eyes gleaming softly in the shadowy light.

'OK, the prologue.' Pia/Hippolyta, from her seat in the 'audience', pointed a directorial finger. 'Go, Quince!'

No director? thought Seph. What a joke.

Her eyes found Annie's; they exchanged tiny smiles.

'If we offend it is with our good will,' started Wez, holding his book out in front of him. He read through Quince's first lines with the assurance of the born actor, already taking on some of Quince's bossy manner. His other hand was held aloft; his voice hung richly in the warm night air.

Perfect casting, thought Seph. If only everyone could be this good.

Quince finished. Pia nudged Simon, who gave a start.

'What – already?'

Pia reached over and jabbed her finger on Theseus's line.

'There.'

Simon read his first line in a cheerful, loud and completely unconvincing fashion.

Seph's heart sank. How on earth was this all going to work?

Then it was Lysander/Sarah's turn.

'Shivers,' she squeaked, staring at the page. 'I thought I hardly had any lines!'

'You don't,' piped up Melissa. 'This one's about your biggest.' She looked down at her book. 'And it's only an aside – say it in a joking kind of way.'

There was a small silence. Lightning snaked into the

treeline across the gully, followed by a small crackle of thunder.

Pia frowned.

'Say it however you want, Sarah.'

Jeez, thought Seph, this is going to be fun.

Sarah took a breath and said her bit. Followed by Pia, speaking Hippolyta's part in high and fluttery tones – out to play the princess for all it was worth.

Seph had to restrain herself from looking at Annie again.

Finally it was time, while Quince said the rest of the prologue, for the entry of the 'players'. Seph shuffled on with Annie, Pak, Jules and Tom; they stood there self-consciously as Quince pointed them out, one by one.

'No, Quince,' called Pia, from the gallery, 'you should *introduce* them, individually.'

'What d'you think I'm doing?' Wez planted his hands on his hips and wiped his sweaty brow. 'I *am* introducing them.'

'No-o!' Pia stood up. 'Each character should take an individual bow, as in –'

She broke off and hurried over. 'Quince should pull out each player, and he or she should bow, according to their *character*.'

She frowned down at her book. 'This man is Pyramus, if you would know,' she read. 'And while he's saying that,' she told Tom, 'you should step forward and do a humungous bow, the way Bottom would.'

Tom stepped forward and awkwardly performed a

sketchy approximation of a courtly bow, arm sweeping out from his waist.

'No-o!' Pia was almost stamping her foot. 'As *Bottom* would! He's a terrible show-off, remember?'

Tom looked at her in silence; Pia made a little noise of frustration.

'As in –' She paused, then, throwing caution to the wind, attempted a pretty good pantomime of the foolish Bottom accepting a standing ovation, chest puffed out, eyes cast heavenward. 'Well, something like that,' she finished, reddening slightly in the ensuing silence.

There was a burst of laughter and applause.

'Really, P,' grinned Simon, 'I don't know why you don't just play all the parts yourself!'

'*And* direct your own performance!' cried Seph.

More laughter; Simon and Seph's eyes met. And a small thrill went through Seph; a tiny ripple of delight.

He finds you amusing – Pia's Big Hero actually finds little ol' you amusing.

Her gaze dropped to his hands, so large, the hairs on them so fair. The hands that held her in the dream . . .

'Well, someone's gotta help things along!'

The laughter died; everyone looked at Pia. She was standing there, looking reproachful. To put it mildly.

Finally she took an enormous breath and shrugged, exaggeratedly.

'Well, somebody *else* do it then! I'm only trying to get things going. *Anybody* is welcome to contribute.'

Oh yeah? Seph didn't dare glance at Melissa.

Pia suddenly looked as though she was about to cry; people sprang to reassure her.

'Oh, P,' said Simon, throwing his arm around her shoulder, 'Ba-by! We were only joking.'

'You're doing a *great* job,' cried Sarah.

'We'd be lost without you!' added Jules.

Wez fell to his knees, seizing her hand in both of his.

'Please, Pia – we *need* you to direct us!'

Pia, looking slightly mollified, wrenched her hand away and made a face at him.

Seph looked at Melissa. She was sitting there, arms still folded, not saying a word.

But I haven't said anything either, Seph thought.

'So,' said Simon, squeezing Pia's shoulder, 'you be director, okay?'

'Well . . .' Pia was trying hard not to look too pleased. 'I guess, if you really think –'

'From now on,' declared Annie, one finger raised, 'it's Pia slash Director slash Hippolyta.'

She and Seph certainly couldn't look at one another this time.

So now came the part Seph had been dreading – the declarations of love between Pyramus and Thisbe through the hole in the Wall.

First Annie did her speech as Snout, introducing the character as the Wall – hilariously, as Seph knew she would. Seph had once seen Annie playing, of all things, a little boy in a school production, and she'd been a standout.

Now she was portraying Snout as the opposite of herself – a complete idiot.

'And such a wall,' she told the 'audience' earnestly, 'as I would have you think/That had in it a crannied hole . . .' She made a hole by joining the tips of her thumb and forefinger, and pointing strenuously to it, in case anyone missed the point.

Everyone broke up; with her lips puckered forward and her brow knitted in concentration, she looked like a chimpanzee. A talking chimp playing Wall . . .

The corners of Annie's mouth were beginning to twitch; the audience reaction was infectious. But she managed to control herself, and finished her speech to wild acclaim.

'Annie, you're wonderful!' shouted Wez.

'Amaaaazing,' agreed Pia, clapping her hands together, and Seph cried, 'Next stop NIDA! You're wasted just doing the Wall,' she added. 'How 'bout playing Thisbe as well?'

If only . . .

She turned to Pia and made a last-ditch plea.

'I'm going to be *hopeless*.'

Then she turned and caught Tom looking at her strangely. She looked away, willing herself not to alter her expression.

Shit – how on earth did I get bullied into this?

'Nonsense,' said Simon gallantly. 'You'll be great.' He smiled at her, and suddenly it was all too much. Seph gave a tiny, rapid shake of her head and dropped her head to the page, her heart starting to thump.

'Your line, Theseus,' she heard Pia prompt, and Theseus and Demetrius delivered their smartarsed, scornful audience asides. Then Pyramus, aka Tom,

177

entered on the other side of the Wall and, after another remark from Theseus, started his speech.

And he wasn't too bad. His book held high, he deliberately overacted his lines, alternately extending his other arm and clutching it to his chest in a parody of a Shakespearean hero – a kind of idiot, low-life Romeo. His character, Pyramus, was much affeared that Thisbe would be a no-show for their lovers' tryst – to be conducted through the 'hole' in Annie's Wall.

He's enjoying himself, thought Seph; that's what I've got to try and do. Just play the dizzy dame, Seph; no need to make anything personal out of it.

But by the time the moment came for her entrance on the other side of the Wall, her heart was really galloping. Luckily, because she was reading the lines she didn't have to look at him, but her voice came out very thin and high and she ended up completely swallowing the last line.

And when Pyramus sidled up to the 'hole', looked straight at her and cried, 'Thisbe!', she thought she'd die.

She could feel her face beginning to throb. Hardly able to breathe, she buried her head in the book . . .

'My love! Thou art my love, I think?' she managed, in strangled tones. Her voice sounded totally unlike her own; she thought she might faint.

'Slow down a bit, Sephi,' cried Wez. 'You're in love with him, remember?'

The worst – this absolutely *had* to be the worst moment of her life.

Saturday afternoon: postmortem by phone. Seph was sitting cross-legged on her bed with the cordless, her back against the wall; she imagined Pia doing the same.

'Well, I hope to god everyone's learnt their lines by next rehearsal.'

'Doubt it,' said Seph, tucking the phone between her shoulder and chin and inspecting her toenails, one by one.

'Well, at least there's *one* person who'll be sure to know all hers.'

Seph giggled. 'Melissa? *And* everyone else's lines as well!'

'And doesn't she love saying them!'

'And doesn't she love the *sound* of herself saying them!'

'Doesn't she love *herself*, period!'

They spluttered and snorted, but deeper down guilt was nudging at Seph like a small, unpleasant animal. She had a mental flash of Melissa biting her lip when everyone else was consoling Pia; remembered the look of raw hurt in her eyes when Wez'd said that Pia should be director.

The image of that blind man was appearing again. She pushed it away.

'What's Simon like at learning lines, I wonder?' she asked. 'He's sure got a few.'

'God knows.' Pia sighed. 'I mean, he's gorgeous for the part and everything, but . . . well, he's not exactly the world's greatest actor, is he?'

Seph smiled, her chin resting on her knees. 'No, but he's really nice . . .'

On the other end, silence.

'I *mean*,' Seph added hastily, 'he's kind and . . . good fun. Prob'ly makes our lot behave themselves a bit better!'

She thought of what a friend Simon had been to her when she'd finally made it through that dreadful scene with Pyramus. 'Go, Thisbe!' he'd said. 'Doin' a great job, girl!'

And Seph, awash with relief and gratitude, felt like hugging him.

But had Pia, she suddenly wondered, blabbed to Simon about Seph's feelings for Tom? She frowned across at the photo on her desk. Is that why he was being so understanding?

Then she registered Pia's continued silence.

'Yeah, he is nice,' Pia said finally. She paused. 'You two sure seem to get on well.'

Seph felt alarmed, like a weak swimmer who has drifted out of her depth.

'Yeah, well he's really nice to me,' she replied, trying to keep her voice even. But she realised that this made things sound worse. 'I *mean*,' she added rapidly, 'he just seems like a kind person, that's all.'

More silence.

Seph swallowed and took refuge in indignation.

'P, for god's *sake*! As *if* there'd ever be anything between −'

But for a split second she'd had a visit from the dream Simon, putting his arms around her, looking into her eyes. And all at once she'd become almost paralysed with guilt and confusion.

She glanced around and caught sight of her un-opened school bag sitting beside her desk. And imagined her mother, standing there, hands on her hips . . .

'Okay Mum,' she called out to the pretend Susan. 'I'm hanging up now!'

Then, to Pia: 'Mum's on my back. Got a ton of homework. Gotta go.'

Well, the last two statements were at least true.

Later, history book on her lap, staring into space, she heard a car pull up on the opposite side of the street. She craned her head, looking down through the window.

It was the little white car, with Leslie driving; she backed into an available space opposite. She and Ken climbed out, looking casual and relaxed, as though they'd been out for lunch. But as Ken opened the gate and paused to let Leslie go first, Seph saw him glance quickly at their house.

And his suddenly furtive, almost greedy expression was just about the opposite of casual and relaxed-looking.

piachicki <can you bring bean to rehearsal fri night, plees annie??>
annidreama <dunno - have to ask her>
sefi_15 <how's she gunna like being a star?>
annidreama <corse i can>

piachicki <she'll love it>

annidreama <she thinks she is one anyway>

sefi_15 <hey this is nice - all on our ownsome like this>

annidreama <no boys, no gremlin>

sefi_15 <we shld have our own private room more often>

piachicki <without the gremlin and the others>

piachicki <including melissa>

sefi_15 <ooh, bitchy bitchy>

piachicki <seriously, did u see how she kept trying 2 take over the other night>

Cyber-pause. Seph smiled; she imagined Annie doing the same.

annidreama <anyone else get the feeling she kinda likes tom?>

piachicki <kinda!!!>

piachicki <she's got good taste eh seph>

sefi_15 <ha dee ha HA>

annidreama <1 of these days i might have to have a talk with that boy>

sefi_15 <wot about?>

sefi_15 <don't u bloody well DARE annie>

sefi_15 <DONT U DARE>

Bean seemed to be enjoying herself on Friday night, but Annie was a bit worried about her.

'Don't let go of that lead, whatever you do,' she said to Pak/Moonshine. 'She'll be off in a flash!'

Bean had come on heat, and at such times she was inclined to wander, in search of romance. And on two such previous occasions she'd been successful. Each time there'd been anguished postings of lost dog notices, and each time she'd returned approximately thirty-six hours later, exhausted and (as it quickly became evident) triumphantly pregnant – to mystery partners.

The first time around Annie's family were sure the father must have been a corgi, or a hare, judging by the size of the puppies' ears. The second time around the pups were all so minute, the father could only have been a chihuahua.

'Or a rat,' Annie's mum had said darkly.

Though how a chihuahua could have managed to get at a fox terrier, even a miniature one, is anyone's guess. But, as Annie's dad had said, it could've been worse. It would've been a real disaster if one of the dogs had turned out to be a labrador, or a border collie.

'Why don't you just get her desexed?' someone had once asked.

'Because we keep meaning for her to have proper, fox terrier puppies,' Annie had replied. 'It's just that she keeps running off with the wrong sorts!'

'You're a tart, Bean,' Pak told her now, from his seat beside her on the flagstones. He turned and pointed a finger skywards. 'Just cos it's nearly a full moon!'

Everyone looked across the gully; the moon hung

like a great milky eye above the treetops, splashing her white and glittery tears over everything.

'Hey,' added Pak suddenly. 'We don't even *need* a Moonshine!'

Pia looked at him. 'Duh! The performance is going to be in broad daylight?'

Bean was suddenly distracted by something down in the gully. She sat rigid, one ear pricking sharply forward.

'What is it, Bean?' Tom squatted down, his watch glinting in the moonlight. 'Eh? Some hot hunk down there?'

Pia clapped her hands impatiently.

'Come on!' she cried. 'The scene! We're supposed to be *doing* it next week, in case you've forgotten!'

'How?' asked Melissa suddenly, from her deck chair. 'Just *how* are we going to be ready in time?'

Pia swung around.

'If everyone pulls their finger out and starts being positive – that's *how*, Melissa!'

Touché, thought Seph. But deep down she had to agree with Melissa. How indeed? They'd now, for example, got to the part where Moonshine made his entrance, but Pak was still sitting there, grinning and cracking jokes, seemingly quite unaware that they'd reached his bit. She seriously wondered if they'd manage even one uninterrupted run-through of the whole thing before the big day.

'And people learning their *lines* would be a start!' said Pia. She glared at Tom. 'Not looking at anyone in *particular*, of course.'

Tom took a step backwards. '*Me*?' He grinned and threw up his hands in pretend innocence. 'Okay,' he said contritely, 'I promise. By next rehearsal –'

'The *last* rehearsal!' interrupted Pia. 'By the way,' she added, glancing around, 'Sunday arvo okay for everyone?'

There were several replies in the negative. But Tom seemed determined to finish what he was saying.

'*However*, I'll only learn them,' he said, raising his voice and looking straight at Seph, 'if *Thisbe* promises to learn all hers.'

Seph's heart jumped into her throat. He was smiling at her . . .

No, Seph; he's only testing you, stringing you along.

She made a twisted face and looked away.

'I *know* mine,' she muttered. 'Well, most of them.'

She became aware of Wez looking quickly at her and then at Tom.

'She does too,' Wez said, turning to Seph. 'Don't you, Seph?'

Then to Tom, half jokingly: 'Lay off, boy – don't you bully her!'

Seph felt an almost physical sense of irritation. You lay off, Wez – you're not my knight in shining armour.

Tom shrugged, exaggeratedly, and gave Seph a strange smile.

'Hey, Seph. Would I bully you?'

And Seph couldn't help shrugging, shaking her head – and smiling back at him.

Well, a kind of a smile, anyway.

CHAPTER 13

The doorbell jangled into Seph's dreams the next morning, in sharp, insistent bursts. She frowned and pulled the sheet around her ears.

Only one person pushed the button like that – Hedy. Of course, she was being dropped off after staying the night at Nick's place.

And still it rang, and rang. 'Oh for god's sake!' cried Seph, sitting bolt upright, glaring into the morning. She rubbed her eyes and squinted at the alarm clock: 10.30.

'*Coming*!' she heard Susan cry, her footsteps hurrying to the door. The door opened; the Saab growled off up the street.

'Hi dar –' But Susan stopped short; Hedy was saying something Seph couldn't catch.

'What?' cried Susan, her voice ricocheting up from the front door, through Seph's window. Then: 'Oh *really*!'

Seph sat very still, listening. She heard what sounded like the crackling of cellophane. There was a pause, followed by Hedy's excited, 'Read it, Mum!'

'Oh, for heaven's sake!' exclaimed Susan finally.

Then Seph heard the Brays' front door opening. She looked down through the window, just in time to see Leslie coming out of her front door, doctor's bag in hand.

'Oh – Leslie!' cried Susan. More crinkling of cellophane. 'Good morning!'

'Good morni –' started Leslie, smiling her nice smile. But before she could finish, Susan was off again.

'You could be *just* the person!' Susan cried. 'You're not . . . off to the hospital, by any chance?'

'Nursing home, actually,' said Leslie. 'I usually visit my nursing home patients on Saturdays.'

'Great!' Susan suddenly appeared beneath the window as she hurried towards her neighbour. Seph could see the top of her head – a hint of greyish roots peeped through at the crown.

And the huge bunch of long-stemmed white roses in her arms.

'Would you mind very much giving these to some old dear?' Susan crossed the street and held them out to Leslie, who looked down at them and then up at Susan again with surprise.

'From my ex,' said Susan with a quick laugh. 'A peace offering, but really it'd just annoy me to have to look at them!'

Hedy had rushed to her side. 'No, Mum!' she cried, tugging on Susan's elbow. 'You can't give them *away* – they're beautiful!'

'Hedy,' her mother started, with an apologetic laugh at Leslie, 'I don't really . . . need them, thanks –'

'But they're from *Dad*!' wailed Hedy. 'He asked me to make sure I gave them to you, 'specially!'

Seph's heart was beginning to thump; suddenly it was as though she was ten years old again herself. She had to restrain herself from leaning out of the window and adding to Hedy's protests:

Take them, Mum, please take them!

Tears had sprung into her eyes; she furiously brushed them away.

There was another silence below. Susan looked at Hedy; Leslie glanced from Hedy back to Susan again.

'*I* know,' said Susan at last in a bright voice, 'why don't you have them in *your* room, darling?'

'No!' cried Hedy, stamping her foot. 'Dad gave them to *you*!'

Seph saw Susan and Leslie exchange looks. Susan sighed.

'All right. They can go in the vase by the front door.'

Where you'll barely have to look at them, thought Seph.

She made a mental note to keep their water topped up.

───⟶

Six o'clock Sunday evening. With a mixture of charm, wheedling, bribery and just plain hassling, Pia had managed to get everyone there for the last rehearsal. The Big Performance was scheduled for Wednesday, at school, and judging by the way things were going, there'd almost certainly have to be an extra, emergency session on Tuesday night.

Pak, aka Moonshine, was saying his lines. Accompanied by Bean, noisily, though certainly not on cue. She kept whining and yipping and straining at her lead, and peering intently through the iron railing around the terrace, down towards the the park at the bottom of the garden.

'This lanthorn does the hornèd moon present,' said Pak, holding up the hurricane lamp especially purchased for the Harkness family's one and only (disastrous) attempt at camping years ago.

The olde-style English sounded distinctly peculiar in his staccato Thai accent. How weird was it, thought Seph, that people could become so unlike themselves when they had to perform on stage. Quietish, modest Annie could suddenly morph into an outrageously funny clown, whereas Pak . . . Speedy, streetwise, mover-and-shaker Pak had become completely self-conscious and tongue-tied. And it wasn't because he was playing the character that way.

Pak yanked at Bean's lead. 'Bean, stop that!'

'Bean!' shouted Annie from the sidelines. 'Behave yourself!'

Bean grinned and ducked her head apologetically, wagging her tail. But five seconds later she was at it again, yipping and pulling.

They'd got to the part where the court audience was making fun of Moonshine.

'. . . the man should be put into the lantern,' said

Simon/Theseus. His mouth opened to say the next line, but he dried up.

'Ah . . . ah . . . the . . .'

He squinted down at the book placed strategically at his feet, but Melissa, sitting next to him, was ready with his line, off the top of her head.

'How is it else . . .'

'Ah –' Simon held up an acknowledging finger and finished the line. But when it came to his next little speech he forgot again.

And once more it was Melissa to the rescue.

'It appears,' she mouthed, smiling at him as though at a small child, 'by his small light of discretion . . .'

'. . . that he is in the wane,' Simon continued.

'Melissa,' Pia leaned around from the other side of him, frowning, 'he's never going to learn his lines if you keep prompting him! Even,' she added quickly, 'if you do seem to know the whole play off by heart.'

There was a small silence. Oh-oh, thought Seph, biting her lip. *Oh-oh . . .*

Melissa's mouth dropped open, her expression all injured innocence.

'Well sor-*ree*,' she said. 'I was just trying to *help*!'

She glanced around, looking for support, but no-one returned her gaze. Right now, Seph thought wryly, they'd probably all rather the whole thing failed miserably than give Melissa any encouragement.

'Simon,' said Pia irritably, 'you've just *got* to learn your lines, okay?'

Simon nodded contritely.

Seph wagged a finger at him and cried sternly: '*Bad boy*, Simon!'

And they all started laughing.

Except Pia, who folded her arms and pretended to laugh, her eyes flicking back and forth several times between Simon and Seph.

Melissa seemed to be laughing more than anyone.

It's just a joke, a release of tension, Seph told herself, wiping her eyes. But deep down she was amazed and quite ashamed of her own treachery.

Her eyes met Pia's; she looked quickly away again.

If looks could kill.

'Yeah,' said Annie finally, also glancing at Pia, 'seriously, everyone *has* to learn their lines.'

There were general nods and murmurs of agreement. Followed by a shuffling, awkward pause.

'Gee, it's getting *dark*!' said Jules suddenly.

They gazed across at the almost radioactive-looking reflection of the vanished sun glowing on the treetops. Pak put a finger to his temple.

'Daylight saving ended this morning,' he told her. 'Remember?'

Wez was looking at Pia again.

'Reckon there'll be more than just daylight saving ending,' he said, 'if we don't get on with it.'

Fifteen minutes later the reason — or rather, reasons — for Bean's agitation became apparent.

The first arrived during the scene in which Thisbe

191

was bewailing the death of her lover. 'Asleep, my love?' said Seph in her squeaky Thisbe voice, bending over Pyramus's supine form.

It wasn't easy trying to play a boy who was playing a girl, she thought. They should have got one of the boys to do it – it would've been much funnier.

Anyway, thank goodness Tom's eyes were closed . . .

'What, dead, my dove?

'O Pyramus, arise –'

'You should be kneeling right down,' called Pia from her seat. 'Taking his hand!'

Seph glanced at her sharply, but Pia seemed to be in deadly earnest, completely absorbed in her directorial role.

Oh shit. And my hands are all sweaty.

She sank down beside him, feeling sick.

His right arm was flung over his head; his shirt rucked up, exposing his waist and lower ribs. She reached out and picked up his hand with her fingertips, gingerly, as though it was contaminated. It felt surprisingly smooth and warm. She opened her mouth to say the next line, but her mind had gone to porridge.

'Ah . . .' she mumbled. 'Um . . .'

But she was saved by Bean, who suddenly started barking hysterically. Everyone, including the corpse of Pyramus, turned around to see a whiskery snout poking its way through the gate in the railing.

'Bean!' shouted Annie. She grabbed Bean's lead from Pak. '*Shush*!'

They all stared at the intruder. Who, in complete

thrall to Bean's charms, was whining and pawing excitedly at the bars, tail fluttering like a small flag in a gale.

'Lucky the bars are so close together,' laughed Pia. From his position on the steps on the other side, the dog yipped and twisted and pushed his paws through the rails, but his chest was too broad to squeeze through.

'What sort of a mutt are you?' asked Simon, walking over to the gate and peering down. He glanced back at the hysterical Bean. 'Hey,' he told the newcomer, 'she's a bit short for you, isn't she, mate? Why don't you go after a squeeze your own size!'

The other dog was at least twice Bean's height, with long sturdy legs and a wispy, sandy-coloured coat.

Wez grinned. 'Lost cause, for sure!' He looked back at Bean and shook his head. 'Dunno what you see in Bean. She's hardly the Nicole Kidman of the dog world, is she?'

'I beg your *pardon*!' said Annie indignantly. 'Block your ears, Bean!'

'Talk about love being blind,' laughed Pia. 'Both ways!'

'He's a labradoodle,' said Melissa calmly, walking over to the gate.

Everyone looked at her.

'A *what*?' asked Sarah.

'A labradoodle. A cross between a labrador and a standard poodle.' Melissa peered down at the dog, whose coat glowed softly under the lights of the terrace. 'Although this one looks a bit bigger than the others I've seen at dog obedience.'

The expert as usual, thought Seph sourly.

Annie, having tied Bean to a potted cumquat tree, was rushing over to the other dog.

'Buzz off,' she shouted, stamping her foot and flapping her hands at the interloper. 'Go on – scram!'

There were several protests:

'Oh, Annie!'

'Poor dog . . .'

But the dog looked abashed for about one second, before turning his attention once more upon his beloved.

Dogged, Seph thought. Of course – that's where the word 'dogged' comes from.

And then another suitor arrived. A small, squat bulldog, who proceeded to behave in exactly the same manner as the labradoodle. The two dogs pushed vainly at the gate, tongues hanging out, tails (or stub of a tail, in the case of the bulldog) beating time, their hairy faces suffused with doggy passion.

'From the sublime to the ridiculous,' laughed Wez.

'You got Buckley's, fellas,' said Tom.

Annie was totally unamused.

'For heaven's *sake*!' she cried. 'We'll have half the dogs in the neighbourhood here in a minute!'

'Take Bean away – into a different part of the house,' suggested Pia.

'No,' said Annie, reaching for the latch, 'she'll tear the place down!'

She pushed open the gate, forcing the two dogs to beat an unceremonious retreat to the next step down. But as they turned around again in the direction of

Bean, they caught one another's eye. And all at once comradely solidarity was at an end; they snarled at one another ferociously, their hackles rising.

'Come back, Annie!' everyone shouted. 'Don't go near them – you'll get bitten!'

Bean meanwhile had gone completely round the twist. She yelped and jerked frantically at her lead; the hapless cumquat tree was shaken violently, almost bent over double.

The two rivals started circling one another in a kind of bizarre up-and-down dance on the semi-circular steps, growling savagely. Their teeth were bared, their hackles stiff, the bulldog making snapping motions with his slavering jaws.

'Somebody *do* something!' screamed Pia. 'They'll kill one another.'

Sure enough, from his current position at the top the bulldog suddenly launched himself at his taller adversary's throat. The labradoodle yelped and sank his teeth into the bulldog's shoulder. The two dogs instantly became a screaming blur of muscled hair and flashing teeth, rolling over and over themselves down the steps to the grass below.

Everyone stood there helplessly, mouths open, until a sudden jet of water shot out from beside them, arced over the steps and hit the warring dogs full force.

The gasping adversaries separated and stood there, blinking foolishly in the watery onslaught. Then just as quickly they shook themselves and trotted companionably off across the lawn towards the wider-spaced rails of the boundary fence.

Everyone turned, to see Melissa briskly turning off the garden tap.

'That fixed *them* – for the time being at least.' She wound the hose back onto its rack. 'But they're sure to be back.'

'Melissa,' exclaimed Simon, 'you're a legend!'

Melissa gave a tight little smile.

'Well, that's sure enough drama for one night,' said Sarah shakily.

Jules was staring wide-eyed at the moon. 'Speaking of drama –'

But she was interrupted by Bean, who, romantic hopes dashed, had started to howl piteously.

'Shut *up*, Bean,' said Annie, 'or you'll get a cold shower too!'

Seph took up where Jules had left off. 'Just look at that *moon*!' she cried.

From behind the trees the moon was rising like a great luminous blood orange into a filmy, rice-paper sky.

'What a backdrop,' murmured Annie.

Before their eyes the great crescent was swelling into a half-circle and more.

'It's like . . .' Seph trailed off, unable to put words to it. Across the little valley the lights of houses pricked like lanterns amongst the darkening trees.

'Like a stage set – unreal,' came Tom's voice, just behind her.

Seph spun around; her eyes met his.

'Yeah,' she said quickly, with a tiny smile. She spun around again.

That's exactly what she'd wanted to say.

'Ah, romance, eh, Seph?'

It was Wez, right beside her. She suddenly felt his hand on her back, moving up to her shoulder; smelt the tang of his perspiration.

She quickly moved away; marched over to the rail feeling panicky and disoriented.

'Wonder when the next dog'll arrive,' she murmured, pretending to gaze down into the trees.

Then a truly terrible thought hit her.

What if Tom and Wez were in it together? Both of them pretending to lead her on, then laughing themselves silly behind her back?

She leant against the rail, staring down into the gathering darkness. Across the back lawn white pinpricks of potato vine flowers glowed along the boundary fence; she could just see the outline of the gate leading through into the park beyond.

Surely they wouldn't . . .

'Well, come on,' came Melissa's voice from behind. 'Gaping at the scenery's not helping us get on with the play.'

'Yes it is,' said Annie. 'It's giving us inspiration.'

Seph turned around in time to see Wez wagging a finger at Melissa.

'Quite right, oh clever one.' He put a hand on her shoulder. 'From now on,' he said solemnly, 'I'm with you, one hundred per cent, Melissa.'

Seph glanced at Melissa. Shut up, Wez, she thought, shut up.

But Wez was ploughing right on, like a cheerful steamroller. He winked at the others.

'I just love a woman of mastery, don't you?' Gyrating his body in a parody of a fifties rock star, his eyes blissed-out slits. 'Ooh, a strong woman turns me raaaght on!'

'Get lost, Wez!'

Everyone looked at Melissa; the titters died.

Melissa shook Wez's hand off her shoulder angrily; her eyes suddenly glittered with tears.

'You lot think you're just so *smart*, don't you?' she cried, glaring around at everyone. Her eyes met Seph's; Seph felt an instant stab of guilt.

'So smart, and *funny*, in your little *group*. You think you're so cool –'

'But –' started someone.

'*Melissa –*' cried someone else.

But then they all fell silent; even Bean.

Seph could hardly breathe. Someone should go and put their arm around her.

'We *don't* think we're cool!' protested Pia finally, in amazement.

There were headshakings and murmurings of agreement.

Melissa whirled around. 'Ha!' she cried bitterly. 'Says Miss Ultra Cool herself!' She stared at Pia with undisguised hatred. 'We can't all be so *beautiful* and *wonderful* as you, Miss *Pia*!'

Pia stared back at her, dumbstruck. Everyone was silent. Seph knew she wasn't the only one feeling stricken with guilt.

But Melissa could be so annoying . . .

Bean resumed her doggy lament, even more loudly.

'Oh, stuff the lot of you!' cried Melissa. She pushed through them to the gate and flung it open.

'Melissa,' Annie began, taking a couple of steps towards her. 'Don't go down –'

'You can count me out,' continued Melissa, almost spitting out the words. 'This whole performance is going to be truly *terrible*!'

She slammed the gate behind her and stormed off down the lawn.

Five seconds later they heard the bottom gate click as well. They all looked at one another.

'Someone'd better go after her,' Pia said in a small voice. 'There might be weirdos – in the park.'

Seph stared at her. She was looking quite crumpled, like a popped paper bag.

'How 'bout you going, Simon?' suggested Annie. 'And . . . Tom? You're both kind of . . . neutral.'

'I wasn't meaning to be nasty, honest!' cried Wez, his face stricken.

Annie nodded. 'I know, but she didn't think that.'

'Talk about paranoid,' said Pak, scratching his head.

They were silent again, except for Bean, howling her lament to the moon.

'Well,' said Simon, turning to Tom, 'guess we'd better get going.'

Tom grinned. 'If we're not back in twenty minutes –'

'She's probably killed you,' finished Jules.

Tom followed Simon through the gate; they set off down the lawn, their footfalls dying on the grass.

It was the faint click of the bottom gate that finally did it for Bean. One last yelp and an almighty tug at her lead and her beleaguered hitching post was being uprooted.

There was a tearing sound and a shower of earth and she was off, dragging the cumquat tree behind her.

CHAPTER 14

'She'll catch that tree on something,' cried Annie, sprinting off down the lawn, 'and choke herself!'

'It'll be right,' Pia called after her. 'She'll get rid of it pretty quickly!'

'Anyway,' shouted Seph, 'we'll catch her again in a sec!' But images were flashing through her mind – of Bean hanging by the lead from a rock ledge; Bean, lead and tree all tangled up under the wheel of a car . . .

They pounded across the grass, pulling up at the bottom gate. Seph could see the dark shapes of several cumquat leaves lying on the grass where Bean – and tree – had squeezed through.

'What if that bloody labradoodle gets to her!' Annie fumbled with the latch, close to tears. 'The puppies'd be enormous.'

'She'll just have to have a Caesarean birth, that's all,' said Sarah.

'Anyway,' puffed Wez, 'dogs take ages – y'know . . .

doing it.' He patted Annie's back. 'Don't worry, kid, we'll get to her before he does!'

'Well, spread out!' cried Annie as they poured through the gate. 'Those other dogs wouldn't have gone far, surely!'

Seph thought of the road on the other side of the park, and the cars that came roaring down it, very fast. That's where the houses started their march up the hill, in their suburban checkerboard of gardens and driveways.

They fanned out into the trees, their figures tiny amongst the long straight shadows of the moonlit trunks. 'And get the others on the job when you find them,' called Annie, her voice already faint. 'It'll help take Melissa's mind off things.'

Seph headed off left in the direction of Finger Cove, the little harbour beach down the bottom of the park. To her right Wez's shadowy bulk faded into the darkness.

'Hey, Wez,' she called after him, 'you take the middle of the beach; I'll go to the left.'

'Gotcha!'

She made her way down the hill, keeping close to several more back fences. Glanced longingly up into a couple of brightly lit rooms; in one of them a whole lot of people were sitting round a table, roaring with laughter.

She stared down through the trees; through the forest of trunks she could just make out the glitter of water, and patches of sand glowing silvery white in the moonlight.

Come on, Seph, she told herself, it's only good ol' Finger Cove.

She couldn't count the number of hot, cicada-filled afternoons she'd spent there with Pia, baking on the grass, cooling off in the green water.

Then she thought about the slippery black rocks along this side of the inlet, and the fingering shapes of the mangrove bushes at the bottom of the little headland. Several times in the past while climbing out along the rocks they'd come across syringes and used condoms lying in crevasses or among the bushes.

'People must come here at night,' Pia had commented one day. She'd taken a flying leap onto the next rock, almost slipping on the slimy, tide-stranded weed. 'You don't see that kind of stuff happening here during the daytime.'

Surely she, Seph, wouldn't have to go out among the rocks now . . .

The houses and fences had petered out. An impenetrable tangle of vines and bushes ran up the hillside, like an enormous sheet that had been glittery-dusted with moonlight. If the dogs had gone in there, she thought, they'd never find them.

From across the other side of the park she could hear faint voices. 'Be-ean! Here girl. Be-ean . . .'

She opened her mouth to follow suit, but the sound died in her throat. 'Bean,' she croaked. 'Bean!'

She swallowed. Up ahead stood the big willow tree that overhung a storm drain. So bright and clear in the moonlight; the shadows underneath it so inky black.

Anyone could be hiding under there.

She gave it a wide berth, her heart starting to thump. And as she passed, she was sure she heard something move –

She was positive.

It's probably Bean and her mates – stop! Turn round and call out, you gutless wonder.

No way!

Quite suddenly she was terrified. She took off, bolting through the trees and the stalking shadows, down the hill to the beach, her feet thudding in time with her tearing heart. And then she tripped on a root and fell forward, her hands coming down on sticks and leaves and earth, something sharp scraping her shin. She cried out and scrambled back to her feet as something with wings flitted past, almost brushing her face. It couldn't be a bird . . .

Bat – it was a bat!

She seemed to have stumbled into her own nightmares! She leapt up and flew off again, reason left behind.

And here was the beach. She hurtled into the clear ribbon of sand and stopped dead just out of the shadows, her breath coming in shallow gasps. She stared around at the silent, shining beach, and the moon rippling on the water. And at the nearby shadows, gaping black like caves.

She whirled around again to the water, stared at the red light blinking steadily on its pole out at the mouth of the cove. Where the hell were all the others? And Wez, who was meant to be heading in this direction – where was he?

Call out, she told herself, call out to him. But she

didn't want to bring attention to herself, couldn't get over the sensation of being watched.

You can't stand here all night.

They've probably found Bean, and Melissa, she thought. They'll be making their merry way back to the house, and those lights . . .

How are you going to make it back up through there on your own?

Suddenly, somewhere close by in the shadows, there was a movement. A blur, a scraping sound.

From where exactly?

She took a step forward on the sand, holding her breath, her eyes and ears straining. Surely it was the dogs; please, oh god, let it be the dogs! She stood there, rigid, but all she could hear was her own heart pounding in her ears.

There was a quick step behind her, on the sand –

And then an arm grabbed her roughly round her waist; a hand clamped over her eyes.

Seph instantly became an animal, a screaming, scratching thing of fists and teeth and whipping hair. She twisted and kicked at her attacker's shins, her teeth snapping at the arm pinioning her head. Her fist sank – pow! – into his stomach.

A soft, jelly-like stomach.

'Oof!'

He gasped and let her go. She toppled backwards into the sand and lay there, staring up at Wez, who was clutching at his stomach, doubled over in pain.

'Jeez, Seph,' he muttered, 'who'd ya think I was – Jack the bloody Ripper?'

Seph scrambled to her feet, her shock turning to rage.

'Well what a friggin' stupid thing to do!' She was trembling; she felt like lashing out at him all over again. 'What a bloody *stupid* thing to do when I was dead scared here on my own!'

Wez slowly straightened up; they stared at one another in the moonlight. Seph was still panting; Wez's eyes and mouth were turning into dark Os of contrition.

'Aw, Seph,' he said finally. He stretched out a hand. 'I'm sorry . . .'

He looked like an enormous, anxious teddy bear and for a moment she felt guilty for getting so angry. But she wasn't about to put her hand in his, not considering the way he was staring at her.

'S'okay,' she said with a little shrug and a laugh. 'Sorry I was so . . . violent.'

She took a step backwards, peering up the hill. 'What's going on? Have they found Bean yet? Or Melissa?'

Wez shrugged. 'Dunno,' he said dully. 'I heard them calling, a while back.'

'I'm gunna go and find them.' She took another step up the beach. All at once the shadows simply looked like shadows again, nothing more. Braving the dark spots suddenly seemed a much easier proposition than dealing with Wez.

'Seph –'

But Seph was pointing in the direction of the rocks. 'Think I might've heard a movement over there. Why don't you check it out? I'll give you a yell if I find out anything.'

As she plodded back across the sand she could feel his eyes on her, following her into the darkness.

This time she found the concrete path that wound up through the trees on the other side of the reserve. She felt a lot braver now that Wez was within cooee, although she did skirt right around the looming shape of the toilet block. And somewhere up ahead, towards the far end of the park, she could hear voices calling out to one another. Annie's, it sounded like, and –

A twig snapped, just a little way over to her left, where the bottom of the bush-covered slope met the open grass.

Once again she froze and listened, her heart beginning to race. Told herself not to be stupid. Wez would come running if she screamed.

But how unfair was that?

'Hello?' she cried at last, in a small voice. 'Hello?'

Silence. Then another footfall, and the tearing, shredding sound of someone pushing through vegetation.

'These vines!' came Simon's growl. 'You'd think it was the Amazon jungle, not Brown's bloody Reserve!'

Seph laughed and skipped over to him, feeling quite reckless and giddy with relief.

'Phew, you scared me,' she cried. 'I thought you were a baddy!'

Simon emerged sideways through some thick bushes and came to a halt in front of her, his teeth and blond hair shining as though it was bright daylight.

'Ah, little Sephie,' he murmured teasingly, slinging an arm around her shoulder. 'Would I frighten you?'

'Yep,' she giggled, pressing up against his warmth. His chin was brushing against her hair. Suddenly she felt happy and supremely safe, like she used to with her father when she was little. She breathed in that smell of fresh-ironed cotton . . .

It was the same smell as in her nightmares.

And panic rushed through her, all over again. She tried to pull away, but his arm was holding her firmly.

'Gotta go!' she whispered. She turned her head, slowly and fearfully, knowing what was coming next. Who was going to emerge from the trees –

'Well, well, well,' said Pia, stepping into the moon-light. 'This *is* a pretty sight!'

'Yeah,' said Simon, unabashed. He kept his arm around Seph; she felt his chin brush the top of her head again as he looked at Pia. 'Poor Seph was all scared.'

Pia stared at Seph, her eyes glittering in the moon-light. Seph's shrank back, suddenly terrified.

She hates me. She'd like to see me dead . . .

She gave a final tug and broke free of Simon. Pia took a step towards her; Seph stepped back.

'Yeah,' Seph muttered. She heard herself laugh; a shaky, pathetic little laugh. 'I was shit-scared, actually.'

'Yeah?' said Pia slowly. 'You looked it.'

Seph turned so fast in the direction of the path she nearly overbalanced.

'W-where are all the others? Have they found Bean or Melissa yet?'

'Both,' replied Pia. 'That's what I came down to tell

you.' Her eyes moved from Simon to Seph and back again. 'Although neither of you were looking particularly worried about it.'

Simon looked amazed; Seph almost felt like laughing at the terribleness of it all.

'Aw, P,' said Simon, holding out his hand, 'come *on*!'

'No, seriously,' said Pia. Her voice was suddenly shaking with anger and jealousy. 'Why don't we just get it out in the open? Why don't you two admit –'

'Look, *Pia*!'

Suddenly Seph had had enough. She stepped forward, stuck her face in Pia's.

'Don't be *pathetic*. *You* know who I really like!'

And she turned and ran off, leaving the others to sort it out for themselves.

And the next person she bumped into, literally, was Tom.

She was running through the trees in what she hoped was the direction of the others, and the house. Away from the rocks and the shadows and Wez and Simon and Pia. Away from the nightmares. Please, she thought, away from the nightmares . . .

She hadn't found the path again, but she could hear voices, somewhere up to the left, near the road. She altered her course in that direction, swerved around a big tree and *bang* – she smacked straight into him.

'Augh!'

They both stood there, centimetres apart, staring at one another, the peculiar noise they'd made still hanging in the air.

It was as though she was electrified, she'd had such

a shock. Tears flooded her eyes; she thought she must be winded.

Was this still part of the nightmare, she wondered.

'Hey.' She felt him taking hold of her elbow. 'You okay?'

She tried pulling away, couldn't let him see the tears. He might laugh. They might all laugh.

'No,' she said finally, in a low, strangled voice. 'I'm –' She stopped, then the rest of it came pouring out in a wail: '*No-ot!*'

Tom took her other elbow, then both her hands in his. She tried pulling them away, but he hung on tightly.

Let go of me, she was going to scream, but her throat and eyes were choked with tears; she couldn't even wipe them away. She stood there, her throat aching, feeling as though she was about to suffocate.

'Seph –'

'*What?*' She finally gave an almighty yank and freed her hands, wiping them across her eyes. She stared down at the dark web of grass stretching across the sand.

'Sorry I've –' Tom stopped. He scratched his head and started again. 'Sorry things've been a bit weird lately, between us, but I thought –'

Seph looked up at him; he was frowning with the effort of trying to say what he wanted to. Her gaze slid to a point somewhere over his shoulder.

'What?' she asked again, struggling to keep her voice level.

'Well, Wez really likes you, see, and –'

'*Wez?*' she cried furiously.

They stared at one another.

'Well I don't like *him*,' she said finally, swallowing. 'At least, not like *that*! I mean,' she rushed on, feeling Tom's eyes on her, 'you just couldn't think of Wez as a *crush* – he's just too . . .'

'Fat?' asked Tom quietly, after a moment.

'Yeah.' Seph tried for a little laugh, but she suddenly felt a tiny flood of shame. She sounded so shallow . . .

She looked down at the grass again. 'And . . . Wez-ish!' she said finally. 'I mean, he's a great guy and everything, but he's just not my type.'

It was true; even if Wez had been slim, she could only ever have thought of him as a friend. But someone else would eventually love him, she knew.

They were silent for another moment, then Tom smiled at her and shrugged.

'Well, you danced with him enough – at the social. I wondered . . .' He trailed off, rubbing at his neck; the moonlight glittered in his eyes. 'He reckoned you two were just about an item, then and there!'

'Oh!'

It was as though she'd been winded, all over again. 'As if I had any *choice*!' she cried. '*You* didn't –'

She stopped dead, terrified. But he was taking her hand once more.

'Yeah, well,' he said, 'sorry.' He leant in towards her; their foreheads touched.

Seph could hardly believe it; this must be all still part of this ridiculous, crazy dream she was having.

But his arms sliding around her felt real enough. 'Guess it seemed all too much of a hassle at the time – to upset a mate,' he murmured. 'By getting with you.

But I've really liked you, ever since that day at the beach.'

Seph's heart and throat were so choked she couldn't make a sound.

'Forgive me?' He pulled her closer.

Too much of a hassle, a tiny voice was screaming somewhere in her head. What about all the hassles you've caused *me*?

But then they were kissing, and she forgot all that.

CHAPTER 15

The following Wednesday afternoon it was back to Cappo's again, for an impromptu cast party after the Big Performance. And things were getting a bit hysterical.

'Well at least Bean behaved herself,' cried Annie, wiping her eyes.

'No other dogs at St Anne's,' added Pia. Then instantly realised what she'd said and made a face.

'Of the canine variety, at least!' shouted Wez and Pak on either side of her, almost in unison. Pia jabbed them hard with her elbows; they doubled over, laughing.

'Well, what about when I had to go and pick her up at lunchtime?' said Simon. He pointed at Annie. 'I let myself in through your side gate and scooped her up. She was barking hysterically, and Tom's grandmother next door thought I was *pinching* her!'

The thought of anyone wanting to steal Bean set

them all off again. They gasped and stamped their feet under the table.

'The phantom Grammar dog-napper!' said Wez.

'Must give her a hard time about it tonight,' laughed Tom.

Bean, chained to the lamppost outside, cocked an ear and barked at them through the door. They were sitting inside today; there was a certain autumnal chill in the air.

'Okay, Bean,' called Annie. 'Only a little bit longer.'

'Hey, Bean,' shouted Wez, 'any more coitus interruptus lately?'

Bean had been found just in time that night in the park; the bulldog was about to do his worst.

'*Shoosh*!' They leant forward, giggling, hunching their shoulders. People at other tables glanced their way, again.

'We'll be thrown outa here,' spluttered Seph, starting to choke. She banged down her mug; hot chocolate slopped onto the table.

'Any minute,' agreed Leonie cheerfully, squeezing past. She leant forward, mopping up the spill with her cloth.

'Here,' said Annie, passing her water glass across to the coughing Seph, 'have a drink.'

Seph grabbed it and took a swig, to a chorus of smart and/or concerned remarks.

'Okay?' asked Tom. He patted her on the back, then slid his arm around her shoulder, his face next to hers. 'Hey?'

Seph nodded, her eyes streaming. Her face, she knew, must be puce-coloured.

She tried to smile at him, suddenly remembering their last visit to Cappo's. That afternoon had marked the start of a kind of colossal bad dream. She wouldn't have believed the way things had turned out . . .

And now it was Wez's turn to hide the hurt. She was aware of him quickly glancing at her and Tom, his wisecracking grin crumpling very slightly at the sight of their two heads close together. Been there, done that, she thought with a sudden sad rush of affection for him. She knew just what he'd be feeling at this moment. Giving himself a mental shake, forcing himself to rejoin the conversation.

She would have liked to reach over and give his hand a squeeze.

The talk was returning to the performance.

'Hey,' cried Jules, 'what about when Wez started *spitting*, all over Mrs Ahern in the front row!'

There were shouts of '*Yes*!' and 'God, that was funny!'

'Me – *spit*?' asked Wez, his face lighting up again. 'Never!'

'With bloody, blameful blade,' quoted Pak, his lips protruding, Daffy Duck style. 'What was it? *He –*'

'– bravely broached his boiling bloody breast,' finished Wez, spraying them all over again, to howls of protest.

'She actually got out her *hanky*,' laughed Pia, 'and wiped her face, you were spraying so hard – I saw her!'

What with the choking and the laughing, Seph's stomach muscles were beginning to seize up.

'You're disgusting, Tupper Ware,' said Tom. 'Can't take you anywhere.'

'She was . . . *touched* by my comic genius, that's all,' Wez cried, his plump arms gesturing theatrically.

'Literally!'

'Well, you *were* bloody hilarious, Wez,' said Seph, grinning at him.

Hearty agreement all around: 'I'll say!' and 'Yay, Wez!'

'You're a legend, old son,' said Pak, clapping him on the back. 'What would we do without ya?'

'Please, oh please,' said Wez, waving a mock-humble hand, but Seph could see him flushing with pleasure.

'Well anyway,' chimed in Melissa suddenly, 'I reckon she would have given us a good mark for it.'

Trust you, Melissa, thought Seph, smiling wryly. We had all five Year 10 English classes on the edge of their seats, laughing their heads off, and all you can think of is marks.

But that was our Melissa, she decided. Someone had to care about things like that. In the end it had been Melissa who'd become the self-styled props and wardrobe mistress, organising outfits and making sure that crucial props were there when needed.

She seemed to have calmed down pretty quickly when they'd finally all made it back to the house from the park that crazy night. Pacified, Pia had said later, by the idea of everybody out looking for her. Although she hadn't looked exactly thrilled when Tom and Seph arrived back together, last of all, smiling and a bit flushed.

And as for Wez . . . Seph could hardly look at him. But she knew he was definitely having a hard time playing his normal, clown-like self.

Now she stared at Melissa. You're a complicated number, she thought. Melissa's gaze darted about, waiting for her chance to add something weighty to a totally unserious conversation. And she never, Seph thought, seems to really laugh, not proper belly laughs anyway.

Melissa, she decided, could be full of surprises.

———␣⊃

'For the last time,' said Tom, holding up his hands, 'I am *not* the gremlin, okay? Never have been, never will be!'

'Nah, of course not,' leered Pak, leaning around Seph. 'It's just coincidental that the ol' grem's always online when you aren't!'

'And vice versa,' said Seph, smiling sideways at Tom. He made a face at her and put a pretend fist up to her nose.

Although now she'd got to know him better, she really didn't think it was Tom. She had her own suspicions on that subject. Not that the gremlin had appeared lately. He/she hadn't had much chance; everyone just seemed to have been too busy for many online chats.

It was a Saturday afternoon; they were marching down Whitechapple Road to the cinema. To see some French movie Annie said was meant to be really good.

About love, and being French. The boys said they were walking out if it got too mushy.

It was just the old gang again. Not Simon; his mid-years were getting too close, Pia had said with a small frown. Even though the break would've done him good.

Seph hadn't clapped eyes on Simon since that afternoon at Cappo's; even Pia had only seen him once or twice.

'Probably put off by our juvenile behaviour,' Pia had murmured in maths the day before. Then she shrugged. 'Oh well, let him be Mr Maturity – who cares?'

You care, thought Seph, watching Pia as she turned back to her page and, chin in hand, absently resumed her doodling. You care heaps, Pia.

And she did seem awfully quiet today, for Pia. Seph sneaked a sideways look at her friend. Pia's arms were wrapped around the front of her thin cardigan; her shoulders were hunched against the breeze. She hasn't got enough clothes on, thought Seph, for this time of year.

A sudden gust scattered some leaves and swirled a sheet of newspaper into the air. But Seph didn't want to think too deeply about Pia's romantic hassles; she'd been there too recently herself.

Seph moved closer to Tom; they laced their fingers together, their feet stamping along the pavement. But she couldn't quite keep time with him; their strides didn't seem to match.

Sometimes, she'd come to realise, it was a bit like that with their conversations, too. They didn't really think the same about a lot of things . . .

She pushed the thought from her mind.

Then, out of the corner of her eye she saw the blind man, sitting there on the same stool in front of the construction zone, his ancient, synthetic-looking cardigan all scuffed and pilled and . . . slippers on his feet. His face was tilted upwards, his expression that strange and rather radiant mixture of blankness and hopefulness.

'Hey, Annie.' Seph stopped, nodding in his direction. 'Look.' She fumbled with the latch of her bag. 'Hang on, everyone. Gotta buy a pen.'

They all stopped and looked at her, then at the man. Seph glanced at him quickly, but he showed no sign of having heard.

Annie and Pia started digging in their bags and Wez felt for his wallet. But the other two weren't keen.

'Don't need any pens,' muttered Tom.

'If you gave money to every begg –' started Pak, but he stopped short, frozen by Seph's glare.

She could have strangled both of them.

She found the five dollar note she had tucked away behind her library card, for emergencies. There goes my movie Coke and icecream, she thought. She walked over to the man and bent down in front of him.

'Hi,' she said, gently touching his hand. 'I'll have five pens, thanks.' She gave a little laugh. 'I'm always losing them!'

They were actually the cheap kind Seph hated; thin and scratchy and prone to drying up too quickly.

The man tilted his head a fraction, but his gaze remained fixed, his eyes milky. She could smell the pungent odour of old man, of leathery skin and unaired clothes.

'That's very kind of you,' he said finally, in a voice strained and lacking resonance, like a neglected piano. 'But I'm sure you don't need five of them.'

His smile was slight, faraway. Almost, Seph thought suddenly, as though he could hear an angel singing, somewhere distantly.

'Oh yes I *do*,' she cried, pushing the note into his hand, 'you don't know me!'

'Well, thank you.' He inclined his head, making a slight gesture in the direction of the pens. 'Please help yourself.'

The veins in his neck stood out above his frayed collar; his skin had a bluish tinge.

'And I'll have three,' said Annie, stepping forward.

'Me too,' said Pia. Followed by Wez, and then, of course, the other two.

'This is more,' said the old man, 'than I've sold the whole of the past two days.'

They looked at him in silence.

'Please.' He gestured again. 'Help yourselves.'

Seph took only one pen; the others followed suit.

'No,' said the man, still gazing outwards, 'please take the whole number you've paid for.'

A prickle ran fiercely up the back of Seph's neck; she thought she might cry.

'Are you,' she started, squatting down. 'I mean . . . who comes to collect you?'

He was silent for a moment, before inclining his head again.

'My nephew, or some other kind friend, usually.'

Seph tried to picture the nephew and other 'friends' who could leave an old man sitting there all day on his own.

'We could –' she started. 'I mean, would you like –' She broke off, registering the boys growing restless behind her.

His other hand touched hers, surprisingly warm for the dry, papery feel of it.

'No,' he said, 'you must be on your way.' The smile increased, almost imperceptibly. 'Where are you all off to?'

'A movie,' they chorused, Pia adding, somewhat ridiculously: '*Une Rose D'hiver.*'

But the old man nodded. And said, amazingly: 'I've heard that's meant to be good.' There was another trace of a smile. 'Enjoy.'

'Hey, man,' said Pak admiringly, 'stay cool.'

'And you,' said the blind man, nodding solemnly.

Seph reluctantly straightened up, but as they were turning to leave, she swung around once more.

'Hey,' she said, 'I'm Seph. And this is Annie, Pia, Tom, Wez and Pak.' She swallowed. 'We'll stop by and say hi again, if you like, really soon.'

The old man inclined his head once more. 'Thank you,' he said gravely. 'I'd like that, very much.'

As they were standing waiting near the candy counter, Pia gave Seph a nudge.

'Look,' she said, nodding across the foyer, 'over there.'

Seph looked in the direction Pia was indicating and saw a boy grinning at her through the crowd. And this time she recognised him straight away.

She grinned and gave a little wave back.

'Cute,' murmured Annie. 'Who is he?'

'Oh,' said Seph, taking a step in his direction, 'just this guy I keep bumping into . . .'

Seph and he made their way towards one another through the crowd.

'Hey,' he said, stopping. 'Hello again.' He grinned. 'Your dad still spouting Shakespeare?'

Seph rolled her eyes, warmth spreading through her in a rush.

'Yeah,' she said, 'so embarrassing . . .'

She couldn't believe he remembered her.

Or maybe it was just Nick who had stuck in his mind.

'You're lucky,' he said. 'My old man would know precisely zilch about Shakespeare. Or anything much else for that matter,' he added with a shrug.

'Oh . . .'

He must, she thought, registering his sparky eyes and the beads at his throat, be a total reaction against his dad.

'Hey,' he said, 'I'm Zac.'

'Seph,' said Seph.

They stood there, still smiling at one another. Zac glanced vaguely over her shoulder.

'You here with anyone?'

'Oh . . .' Seph waved an equally vague hand behind her. 'Friends . . .'

'Yeah,' Zac started, 'me t –'

Suddenly Tom was there at her shoulder, bearing two Cokes. Looking at Zac and then at her.

'Hey, Seph,' he said, giving her her drink. 'We're all going in now.'

'Oh.' Seph glanced quickly at Zac. 'Okay –'

'Hi,' Tom said to Zac, 'I'm Tom.'

'Zac,' said Zac, sketching a tiny wave.

Seph suddenly wanted to giggle; they reminded her of those two dogs that night at Pia's, just before they'd hurled themselves at one another's throats.

There was a small silence. People poured around them, heading for Cinema Two.

'Well,' said Zac to Seph. 'Might see ya round.' He grinned. 'At Renny's, maybe?'

'Yeah,' said Seph, smiling back, feeling the colour rising in her face. 'Maybe . . .'

She had to stop herself from adding: Hopefully!

Sunday afternoon, and the homework couldn't be put off any longer. More particularly, the final assignment on *A Midsummer Night's Dream*.

'It'll be good practice,' Mrs Ahern had said ominously, 'for the exams.'

Seph sighed and looked at the sheet; it was one of those 'either/or' essay questions. The kind that when you were halfway through one answer, you'd realise you should've chosen the other:

In roughly 1000 words, comment on either of the following quotes in relation to *A Midsummer Night's Dream:*

> *The course of true love never did run smoothly*
>
> OR
>
> *Lord, what fools these mortals be!*

The blank screen stared back at her; the cursor flashed. She picked up the book and fanned through the pages; they fell softly back into one another, thick and yellowing. How many more girls would read this copy, she wondered, before the school saw fit to buy a new batch?

The course of true love never did run smoothly.

That certainly wasn't a hard one to answer. Helena and Demetrius, Hermia and Lysander, and Oberon and Titania, for that matter, all going through their horrible hassles, before everything was finally sorted, and they all lived happily ever after.

Presumably.

Seph tried to imagine Helena five or ten years hence. Would she be starting to get fat? Would she and Demetrius be taking one another for granted? Would they have produced at least one truly obnoxious kid?

Maybe they might even have ended up getting divorced. She was sure Nick and Susan were madly in love when they got married.

And here *she* was, at last going out with the object of her own heart's desire, and suddenly she couldn't stop thinking about Zac!

True love. Ha ha.

Then she thought of Annie's mum and stepfather, or even Pia's parents.

Perhaps one day . . .

She glanced at the Net icon on the bottom of the screen. Maybe she should just quickly log in and see if Pia was in there; engage her in a little private chat, just happen to mention Zac . . .

No, Seph, no. Remember what happened last time you blabbed?

But what had happened, exactly? Those whole few weeks now seemed a nightmarish blur of jealousy and paranoia and wild imaginings, the details of which, like some horrendous tummy bug, were best forgotten.

Lord, what fools these mortals be . . .

And anyway, Pia would just want to yak about what was happening, or rather, not happening, with Simon.

She could've written a *three* thousand word essay, on either of the topics, about their own lives!

Later, when she'd written about half (she was proud of herself – she'd actually chosen the second, harder question), the phone rang. Hoping against hope (how could Zac possibly have her number?) she snatched it up, but it was only Nick. He often rang about this time, after he got home from his usual Sunday afternoon session at his chambers.

'Seph?'

'Oh hi, Dad –'

'How're things?'

'Pretty good. You?'

'Great.' She could hear him smiling; she realised she was starting to smile too. 'Lisa's here with me,' he continued, 'and we've just decided we're fed up with all this work – we're going on a cruise to Alaska!'

'*Alaska*?'

'Yes, what's wrong with Alaska?'

'Nothing.' But Seph was starting to giggle. 'It just sounds . . . funny, that's all.'

'I can't think why.' Seph could hear laughter and some scuffling going on in the background. 'For your information, missy,' Nick continued, mock-indignantly, 'I've always had a hankering to see Alaska, and so, it turns out, has Lisa.'

'Oh,' said Seph, 'well I hope you have a great time. When are you going?'

'In a couple of weeks. We're dropping everything and taking off. Flying to Vancouver and catching the ship from there.'

'Half your luck!' Seph leaned back in her chair and sighed exaggeratedly. 'Just remember me in the middle of my exams!'

'We'll try to,' said Nick. 'Wish you were coming too . . .'

Like hell, thought Seph wryly.

Then: what if they come back married or something?

'So anyway,' he asked, 'how's Hedy?'

'Good.'

'And Mum?' The question sounded polite and quite disinterested.

'She's fine. Hey, Dad?'

'Mmm?'

Suddenly she felt compelled to set the record straight. 'I – I don't think there really is anything going on between her and Ken.' Seph frowned at the dog-eared book in front of her. 'I think Hedy – Hedy and I – were probably just getting a bit . . . carried away.'

There certainly didn't seem to be anything going on now, at any rate. A couple of weeks ago, when Seph had been setting off up the street and Susan had happened to come out of the front door with her in order to hurl Nick's wilting roses in the bin, they'd met Ken, coming out of his door. There'd been a hint of embarrassment in the air; both Ken and Susan had seemed slightly guarded, as though each was actively wanting to discourage the other.

'Fine,' said Nick, cheerfully. Seph could almost hear him shrugging.

'Although what your mother gets up to is entirely her own concern.'

Later, when Hedy had taken the cordless to her room and Seph was tapping away once more, Hedy re-appeared at the door.

'Seph,' she said, holding the phone to her chest, 'Dad wants to know if they're going to be able to see us both before they go – next weekend, maybe?'

Seph didn't have to think about that one for very long.

'How about taking us for breakfast next Sunday?' She grinned. 'At Renny's.'

―――――⊃

After that her fools and mortals inspiration seemed to have dried up, so she went and parked herself in front of the telly – just for half an hour, she told herself.

It was *The Nanny*. She stared at the screen, vaguely registering that she'd seen this episode (and all the rest of them for that matter) before. But she was really somewhere else altogether; her thoughts banged and rattled about like stray coins in a tumble dryer.

Would Zac be there?

Oh please yes. Oh please no.

Did he normally work there on Sundays?

Hope so. Hope not.

Surely he'd be going out with someone?

Probably, but then so are you!

And: Does he like me, or is he just nice like that to everyone? He's an actor, after all . . .

The Nanny had segued into the news. Then Hedy announced that she was hungry, so Seph heated up the lasagne Susan had left for them (she'd gone out to dinner with friends), even though Seph wasn't the least bit hungry. And before she knew it, some miniseries about World War II was starting and Seph knew it was now or never for her essay.

And then the phone rang again.

'Hey,' said Pia, 'where've you been? Log on, for crying out loud.'

'But –' Seph sighed. 'Oh, okay.'

'Hedy,' she said sternly, tapping her watch as she headed for the stairs, 'as soon as you've finished that, go and clean your teeth and off to bed!'

'Dessert first,' said Hedy indignantly, 'I haven't had my icecream!'

'All right – as soon as you've had it. And only a small bowl.'

'Oh,' pouted Hedy, 'why just a small bo –'

'A medium bowl then!' Seph shouted. 'Just get to bloody *bed* for crying out loud!'

And Seph climbed the stairs as Hedy scuttled for the fridge.

—◝

Ten minutes later:

sefi_15 <gtg - finish this essay>
sefi_15 <else i'll be in deep shit>
piachicki <so - we can be in it deep together>
tupper_wez <wots the topic>
piachicki <i havent even started mine>
tupper_wez <itll be on the net sumwhere>
sefi_15 <'lord wot fools these mortals be'>
annidreama <clueless is on tonite>
tupper_wez <easy - just write about pak n tom>

But here was Tom, on the private screen.

ToMtOm <hey seph wanna go . . .

But something was drawing Seph's eye back to the main screen. Sure enough:

<hey> she typed quickly to Tom, <look whos arrived>.

She stared as the offending name started moving up the screen, quicker and quicker as the others registered his presence and went on the attack. But she knew no-one would put the gremlin on 'Ignore' straight away; they were too intrigued . . .

Tom jumped back to the main screen.

ToMtOm <see - IT AINT ME>

Everything went quiet for a moment.

grEMLin <hey pia hows your boyfrend>

If she had voice chat, Seph knew, Pia's reply would've been a loud scream.

annidreama <its u, isnt it melissa>
piachicki <what do U know about him??>
grEMLin <melissa whose melissa?>
p_a_k <ok then wots his name????>
grEMLin <it starts with s>
piachicki <either tell me or PISS OFF>
grEMLin <ive put a spell on u pia, a potion>

Tupper_wez chimed in with something, but Seph was staring at the last line.

She'd heard that somewhere before, and not so long

ago. Seph suddenly thought of that Harry Potter book, beside Hedy's bed.

In a flash she was out of her chair, through the study door to Hedy's room. She stood there in the doorway, peering into the half light. Her eyes swept over Hedy's familiar treasures: the sheep skull grinning hollowly from its home among the fossils and dried cicadas on top of the bookcase, the Harry Potter book sitting under the lamp, Dog sitting on the pillow . . .

But just as she'd thought, no Hedy. The bed lay flat and undisturbed. The shadowy, weird-shaped faces from *The Simpsons* smiled mockingly back at her from their pride of place on the doona cover.

Even before she'd gone through Susan's door Seph heard the clink of a spoon on china. Hedy was still eating – she must've had a huge helping of icecream.

The room was dark, save for a faint glow emanating from down behind the far side of the bed, near the floor. Which illuminated the top of her sister's head, sticking up just above the edge.

And then it started; the faint but unmistakeable clicking of a keyboard.

Seph tiptoed very quietly across the room; stopped at the bed. The head remained motionless, the shoulders hunched over the task at hand. The clicking paused, started again, then stopped. A hand reached sideways to the spoon . . .

Seph let out a roar and hurled herself onto her stomach across the bed, clamping her hands round the base of Hedy's pyjama-collared neck.

Hedy screamed; the spoon went flying across the

room. A large blob of icecream plopped onto the rug, narrowly missing the laptop.

'Hedy!' Seph hissed savagely. 'You little –'

'It wasn't me!' cried Hedy. Her hands spread out like starfish in an attempt to cover the screen. 'I was just . . . in another chat room!'

'Ha bloody *ha*!' cried Seph.

They both stared at the laptop; in the gaps between Hedy's plump, texta-stained fingers the mute squawks of Seph's friends were clearly visible scrolling up the screen.

'Out of the way!' Seph grabbed the laptop, placing it in front of her on the doona.

'W-what are you doing?' Hedy twisted around, her eyes huge.

Seph ignored her.

<Hey everyone – seph here – drama over> she typed quickly.

She pushed 'Caps Lock'.

<GREMLIN DISABLED>

'Seph?' asked Hedy a little later, when things had calmed down a bit.

'Mmm?' Seph reached over to switch off Hedy's lamp.

'I didn't mean . . .'

Seph looked down at her sister. Hedy's face, sunk back into the pillow, looked as round as one of those sunflower baby pictures.

'What, Hed?'

Hedy's brow furrowed; she took Seph's other hand in her warm fingers.

'I wasn't meaning to make you upset.' Her lower lip drooped. 'I was just having a bit of fun.'

Some fun, thought Seph. It certainly hadn't been much fun for Hedy's victims.

She stared into the green eyes, shining so beseechingly in the lamplight. Weird, she thought, how one little kid could create such turmoil. It was as though they'd been put under some kind of cyber-sorcery.

'S'okay, Hed.'

She bent down and brushed Hedy's forehead with her lips, breathing in the bedtime aromas of warm skin, flannelette, and Dog, perched beside the pillow.

The arms came around her neck and held her tight.

Seph smiled. 'Just don't do it again, okay?'

Hedy shook her head; Seph could feel her smiling too.

'Night, Seph.'

'Night, Hed.'

And Seph reached up and switched off the light.